To YAL. For getting me to write, even when I might not have always wanted to. Thank you.

CHAPTER ONE

"Hey," Christopher said with a dismissive nod. "What's up?"

The girl stared up at him from her seat, her face pale, her eyes wide. But she said nothing.

Her reaction threw the boy off his game, flustering him ever so slightly. He'd never just been... *looked at*. Laughed at, sure. Told to get lost, a few times. But never simply stared at.

"Uh, is that a ladder in your tights or, uh..." He cursed himself for forgetting the end of the chat-up line. When he realized she wasn't even wearing tights beneath her skirt, he cursed again.

Still she stared.

Clearly not a fan of cheesy opening lines. "I kind of like your freckles," he tried. "They're like tiny grains of sand ironed in by golden sunlight." There, that sounded better. Almost Shakespearean. *Probably*.

No reaction. Just those huge eyes that seemed to stare right through him.

Enough was enough. Christopher waved a hand in front of her face. *"Hello? Anyone home?"*

The girl blinked. "You can *seeme,*" she said slowly. It was more of a statement than a question. "You can, can't you?"

Christopher looked around, wondering if she was in fact talking to him — but the bus was otherwise empty. He could feel his cheeks burning. *Come on Christopher, say something.*

"I uh... Yeah, I got twenty-twenty vision. So don't worry, I can see you just *fine. Can...* can you see *me*?" He winked, hoping more than believing, that the question sounded sexy. Maybe it was at least *flirty?*

"Sit," she hissed.

"Maybe I don't want to," Christopher taunted, his swagger slowly returning.

"*Fucking sit.* Now!"

With a last glance at the empty seats around him, he slid down next to her. "Okay, wow, I guess I can play by those rules."

The girl didn't look at him, instead choosing to stare out of the window at the rolling hills beyond, dyed a lazy orange by the low sun. "What time is it?" she asked without looking away.

"Do you mean..."

"*The time. On your watch.* I think it's a question even *you* can handle."

Christopher frowned, half enjoying her playfulness. "Seven-thirty."

"Morning or evening?"

"Uh... morning. *Obviously.*"

"Then why, Christopher, is the sun setting?"

A chill ran down the boy's spine. "How the hell do you know my-"

"Why is the sun setting," she repeated, "if it's the morning?"

"It's *rising*, I'd guess. I mean, I didn't do great at physics but I think I've got that one covered — I only got up like an hour ago. Now tell me, w*ho are you?* Have you been spying on me — do you sit back here and watch me each day? Or... *oh shit,* have you hacked my phone? I mean... I guess I'm flattered..."

He ran a hand through his hair. "But it's a little creepy. And uh, those pictures... well, you should know that's not *my*-"

"It's *setting*. The light is orange not yellow, and it's getting darker by the minute. We're getting close."

Christopher rolled his eyes. "Sure. Okay, the sun is setting at seven-thirty in the fucking morning."

"Why did you get on this bus, Christopher?"

"... Huh? Well, so I didn't miss it. Why else do people-"

"Where's it going?"

"To... to..." *Where the hell was it going?* "I-"

"Listen to me carefully, because this is going to be hard for you to hear. *You died,* Christopher. Your bike was hit by a car this morning. You are dead."

The boy laughed, but a nervousness had crept into his throat. "What is wrong you with you? Why would you say something like that?"

"Touch the back of your head."

"You're pretty messed up, you know that?" he replied, but found himself reaching over his shoulder. His hand trembled as it touched... *hair.* Christopher let out a sigh that quickly turned into a swear as he felt first the wet stickiness, and then below it, a hole that his fingers slid into. They were met by a mushy texture and a sloppy squishing; Christopher wanted nothing more than to vomit.

"What the fuck!" he screamed, as he jumped up and staggered down the aisle. "*What's going on... What's going on... What's going on!?*"

The girl leapt up from her seat, grabbed Christopher's hand, and yanked him back down.

"Do *not* let the driver see you," she said slowly, sternly. "Or you won't even make it as far as purgatory."

CHAPTER TWO

"Are you done yet?" the girl asked.

"Done?" Christopher managed between desperate gulps of air.

"Pretending to hyperventilate. Has it helped much?"

"*Pretending!?* I'm almost"—a deep breath—"suffocating here."

She raised her eyebrows. There was something reassuring about her calmness. "You're not exactly going to die again. That's *very* rare. Just keep quiet and calm."

"I'm really"—another desperate breath—"*dead*, then?"

The girl nodded, her auburn hair falling down in front of her glacial eyes. "Sorry," she replied, brushing the loose strands out of the way, "But you kind of, maybe, should have worn a helmet."

Christopher almost laughed. *Almost.*

"Gee, thanks mom."

A shrug. "You're welcome."

There was a moment of quiet as Christopher's panting began to ease.

"Who are you?" he asked. He wasn't certain he wanted to know the answer, but the question burned inside him like napalm. He *had* to know.

"You can call me Cassandra."

"That's nice and all. But *who are you?*"

"Oh. Well, you might know my dad. He escorts people who take the longer journeys. I just make this one, on the rare occasion someone like you has to travel it."

"Your dad escorts people to... *wait...*" Christopher stared at the girl as his mouth drooped open like a drawbridge. She was so pale she might as well have been snow, and the bones behind her cheeks pushed out slightly too far. Unnaturally so.

"Hey, don't look at me like that! I'm not a monster or anything, and neither is my father. He just... has to do it. He does it for all of your sakes, you know. And he's not just a skeleton either, before you ask. I always thought that was dumb. How would his bones move without any tendons to pull them?"

"Death's daughter?" He stifled a despairing laugh. "I tried to hit on Death's daughter?"

"Shh," she whispered. "Keep your voice down."

"How would his bones move... well, that's one question, I suppose, but here's another: how am I *talking,* even though I've got a gash the size of a fist that runs halfway through my head? I don't get it. You say I'm dead, but I feel alive. *I am alive!*"

She considered a moment. "You're not totally dead, I suppose. But you're certainly not alive! You're in between. You stepped onto the bus the exact moment of your death. You're in a state now where you're *both*. Or neither. Flux, we call it."

"What, like Schroedinger's cat?"

"I thought you failed physics?"

Christopher shrugged. "Guess I like cats."

What felt like an icy hand began creeping over his body, as he realized how dark it had become. The final rays of the sun were falling flat over rocky hills. In the distance, he could make out the vague silhouettes of mountains, their peaks like a great crown beneath the clouds.

"So... so let's say, you're right. That"—his fingers slowly traced around his wound—"that I'm dead. Why am I on my way to *purgatory*?"

"You know why. Or, you *will* know — just you've forgotten. Temporarily. It's actually very common. A basic kind of denial."

Cassandra must have noticed the expression on his face because she gave him the first hint of a smile. "Hey, it's okay. Look, you really shouldn't be able to see me — no one should — so... so *maybe* there's been an administrative error or something."

"That can happen?"

"Well, *technically*."

He frowned. "Technically?"

"It's just that, well, it's not happened before. *Ever*. But look, here's what's I'm going to do for you: I'm going to come to purgatory too, and with any luck, I'll be able to persuade The Fool to send you on. Simple."

"Fool? *On?*"

"Yeah. *On*. Heaven, or whatever you want to call it."

"What? Heaven? I could... I could see my..." He tried to swallow back the welling tears, but only snot slimed down his throat.

"*Hopefully*. Like I said, *if* He sends you on. We'll find out soon, but I think you've got a good chance."

"And if he doesn't?"

"Don't worry," she said turning to the window. "We'll cross that bridge *if* we come to it."

7

CHAPTER THREE

"Make sure you don't look back at me when we get up," Cassandra instructed. She was sitting behind Christopher now, leaning over and whispering into his ear. "And whatever you do, do not look at the Driver when we walk past. Got it?"

Christopher nodded hesitantly. "What happens if I do look at the Driver?"

"... You'll miss your stop. That would be an incredibly *bad* thing, because there's only one stop left after."

He took a deep breath. Outside, darkness now reigned unchallenged, and Christopher could only make out a path in front of the bus, illuminated by ghostly white light.

"So, no one's ever seen you before?" he asked.

"Hm?"

"You said no one should be able to see you. And when I came over, you were, you know, *surprised*. Like: 'Oh my God, you can see me? That's so cool! Maybe we can be friends.'"

She tilted her head and looked unimpressed. "I *never* said that."

"It was something like that."

Cassandra rolled her eyes. "I was surprised because Passengers can't see Escorts. That's how it works. We're just here to make sure your journey goes smoothly. No hiccups or accidents, that kind of thing."

"But... I *can* see you."

She shrugged again. "Like I said, I think it may be an administrative error. Look, I'll be honest with you, I've not been doing this for very long. Only a few hundred years and-"

"*A few hundred!?* And that's not long?"

"... that's *really* not long, in the grand scheme. I've only made this journey a dozen or so times."

"Oh. Wonderful. You sound like just the person I need."

"I know what I'm doing!" She paused. "*Mostly.* Look at it this way, we're both learning."

"That's not as reassuring as maybe it sounds in your head."

There was a screech as the bus pulled to a halt. The vehicle lurched and Christopher fell forward, his face walloping the chair in front. For the second time that day, he found himself wishing he'd worn a helmet. Cassandra snickered behind him; he was about to tell her to knock it off, when he heard a hiss. For a dreadful moment, he thought a snake was loose on the bus and yanked his legs up onto his seat. It took him a second to realize it was only the doors opening.

He wondered why, in the middle this bizarre situation, he was even worried about a snake.

A voice like blood gargling over broken glass filled the entirety of the vehicle.

"This is your stop. Take leave of the bus. This is your stop."

Christopher's arms began to tremble and his legs felt like overcooked spaghetti.

"Go," Cassandra hissed. "Now!"

He somehow forced his legs to hold him as he pushed himself up and began stumbling down the aisle. Every step he took, the chill in his spine grew more severe. He turned his head to the window. To the darkness. *He mustn't look at the driver.*

9

Christopher's legs barely moved, and each step was like walking through a swamp with dumbbells tied around his ankles. He forced himself to stare out of the windows, hoping to see something reassuring beyond. Grass, or the moon, or well, *anything*. But there was only terrible, perfectly still, blackness.

He wanted nothing more than to look back at Cassandra — but he didn't dare.

Another plodding step.

Another.

"This is your stop. Take leave of the bus. You cannot stay on any longer," said the voice. There was an added malice to it now. A spitefulness. It was as if the driver was taunting Christopher, daring him to disobey.

To stay.

Something moved outside the window. Was it an animal? Christopher squinted as he tried to get a better look. There it was — two yellow eyes surrounded by a face that was... that was *melted?* The eyes were moving, they were about to lock on to his own — *Oh shit!* He squeezed his eyes hard, as he realized it was the driver's reflection!

"This is your stop. This is your very last chance to leave the bus. You must leave now."

Christopher took a deep breath as he forced one leg forward, then the other. *You can do this,* he told himself. *Come on Christopher, you can do this!*

A smell like rotting eggs whisked together with raw sewage forced its way down his throat as he neared the Driver's compartment. Every braincell he had remaining was telling him to keep his eyes closed... but an unyielding compulsion was beginning to overwhelm him. A deep routed curiosity prevalent in every human: the desire to see the Driver's face.

His head began to turn, his eyes began to open.

A hand pressed hard against his back, shoving him forward. He stumbled and almost tripped as he passed by the Driver, but he caught himself on a metal pole, swinging himself around and onto the steps. Fresh air wafted in through the doors. He gasped, greedily taking it in and letting it chisel away at the weights around his ankles.

With just two large strides, he found himself falling out into the night.

There, on the grassy verge, he bent over, trying — failing — to vomit.

"Well that was close!" said Cassandra a moment later. "*What were you playing at?*"

The bus hissed again, then the engine roared and revved as it pulled away.

"I- I don't even know. Something came over me. *Sorry.*"

"Well, at least you made it, I suppose. Come on, we need to get moving."

In the distance, a barrage of sounds rang out. Laughter and screaming and music.

He recognized the music.

* * * * *

"Come on," Cassandra said as she grabbed Christopher's hand, pulling him towards the base of a nearby hill. Towards the jangling melody. The same music that every carnival seemed to play. It brought back memories for Christopher, of his father taking him to the traveling carnival on those rare nights that were full of excitement and possibilities. When he had that feeling — just for a few hours — that *anything at all* could happen. Because to a kid, at a carnival, anything *could* happen.

"We might as well get this over with," Cassandra continued as she led him up the hill.

"I can manage," he replied, yanking his hand away from hers, but instantly regretting doing so.

"As you wish," she said, falling back to his side.

"Sorry, I- I didn't mean to be rude, it's just that I'm fine and really-"

"It's okay. I get it."

He nodded, hoping she really did 'get it'.

The grass on the hill was coarse and thick, and with each step Christopher took, it tangled around his legs as if trying to keep him for its own. It didn't seem to bother Cassandra who was strolling by his side. If it hadn't been for the fact that he could see her feet treading on the ground, he'd have sworn she was gliding.

"Do you do this for everyone?" he asked.

"What do you mean?"

"Well, you saved me just now on the bus. And, you said you're going to speak to the… uh… *that guy*, for me."

"*The Fool.*" Cassandra sighed. "No, I don't do it for everyone. I would if I could! But Passengers can't see me, can't hear me and they certainly can't feel me pushing on their back. I lose"—a long breath—"many souls on the bus. Some know better than to look. Most, well they just can't resist."

The music was becoming louder and more frantic as they continued up the hill, as if the song was preparing to launch into a tumbling crescendo.

They walked wordlessly for a few minutes as Christopher took in the haunting music and let his thoughts drift back to the final time he'd seen his father.

"Who is this person, exactly?" he asked. "This *Fool?*"

There was no reply.

He turned to Cassandra. Only... *there was no Cassandra.* Just, darkness.

Anxiety swirled in his stomach. He stopped still and turned, but couldn't make anything out in the moonless night, beyond the grass wrapped around his legs.

"Cassandra?" he yelled through cupped hands. "Cassandra! Where are you?!"

As he turned, he noticed two eyes peering out of the blackness to his left, growing larger as they neared him. For a second, he let himself believe Cassandra had returned. But the eyes were too large, too bloodshot.

Next to them, a second pair of eyes flicked open.

Then a third.

Christopher tried to call out for Cassandra, desperate this time, but his voice was lost in his throat, and the few words that did make it out, tumbled softly to the grass by his feet.

Whatever the creature was, it was snarling at him. Hot breath drifted from it like gun smoke, and he finally understood what the term 'blood-curdling' meant. As it stepped ever nearer, he could see it for what it was: a great three headed beast — a huge dog type creature. Its breath stank of decaying meat.

"Cassandra," he mumbled a final time as the mouths opened in unison, revealing row upon row of needle-like fangs. The middle mouth licked its lips in anticipation, as the left and right snapped.

"Oh God."

The beast crouched down on its front legs, its thick, vascular body tense as it readied to leap.

"*Oh God.*"

In the background he could still hear the off-kilter sound of the carnival music, forcing its way through the beating of his heart.

"*Please...*"

It jumped!

13

There was a blinding flash.

The creature fell out of the air mid-leap, landing awkwardly on its side. In a second, it had regained its posture and bellowed out a defiant roar. It readied itself to pounce again.

Cassandra came running out of the darkness, her eyes a flickering burning blue. She stepped between Christopher and the creature.

"**No,**" she said defiantly. "He is with me." Her voice was somehow many voices now. Light crackled from her palms as she raised them. "If you wish to take him, you will need also to take me."

The central head roared again, but its counterparts whimpered. It snapped at the left, then the right; they bowed their necks in shame and stared down at the grass like wilted flowers.

The middle head let out a final roar before it bared its teeth at Cassandra. Then, the monster stepped backwards, back into the darkness it had come from.

"Stay by me now," she instructed. Her eyes simmered back to their familiar deep blue, and her voice was... just a *voice*.

"Wh- what was that?" Christopher asked, his voice shaking almost as much as his arms.

"I'd guess it's a creature from The Carnival. I've seen some like it before."

"Would it have killed me? Like, *again*?"

"No... But what it would have done would have been worse."

She held out a hand.

Christopher hesitated a second before reaching out.

"Where did you go?" he asked, as they ascended the hill.

"I didn't."

"Well, you weren't next to me when I looked."

"You wandered off, Christopher. I found you halfway down — back where we'd already been."

Christopher frowned. "I don't think so."

"I know so. It's not your fault, though. The creature lured you."

"What?"

"One of the heads confused you. We wouldn't have even heard it, but"—she tapped her head—"it would have messed with you in here. A high pitched whine that disorientated you."

"I… *Oh*. Well, thank you."

Cassandra smiled, and from there they walked silently until they reached the hill's summit. Christopher gazed down onto a puddle of multicolored light far below, surrounded by the crown of mountains he had seen from the bus.

It was an ocean of activity. Of lights, of noises, and smells that drifted up to them.

It was indeed a carnival.

But this wasn't like any of the carnivals his father had ever taken him to.

This was a carnival for the dead.

CHAPTER FOUR

"Come on, Chris," said Markus, handing his son a sloppy slice of pepperoni pizza. "What's the matter? You usually love this place."

Screams and laughter rang hollow in Christopher's ears. It was true, he did *usually* love this place. When he'd been a kid. But he was fifteen now and the moaning ghosts of the haunted house had all but lost their luster. They sounded mechanical. Fake. The smells of hot oil and sugar and excitement had been replaced with the far more real stench of nicotine mixed with sweat and vomit. The pizza tasted of grease.

"I'm too old for it, dad."

"What do you mean, *it*?"

"You know what I mean. The coconut shy. The ghost train. The ferris wheel. *The carnival*, dad. All of it."

Markus's smile wavered for half a second. "Come on! No one's too old for the carnival. Look at me, I still love it and I'm in my forties!"

His dad loved it, because he was more of a kid than Christopher had ever been. More immature, that's what his mother liked to say. A party machine still more fond of his wine than of his family. That's why they'd split up too, his parents, and why he only saw his dad the amount of times a year that he could count on one hand.

"Come on, I know what'll cheer you up," Markus said, as he swallowed down the last of his slice.

Christopher let out a long breath as he followed his father. The usual carnival music blared out tunelessly somewhere in front of them.

"Hear that?"

"Yeah..."

"It's called Entry of the Gladiators. Can't you just see two warriors strutting out into the amphitheater, their swords held high in their hands. The crowd going wild, baying for blood! For Sparta!"

Chris could *not* see it. He could only see a poorly trained clown standing outside the funhouse, attempting to juggle, but spending as much time picking up balls from the ground as he did throwing them up into the air. Multi-colored lightbulbs flashed erratically around the funhouse's entrance. Once every three or four bulbs, a dead light would break up any attempted pattern. If there were any patterns.

"Sparta was the Greeks, dad."

Markus pretended not to hear.

The sign above the funhouse's door had been graffiti'd to read '*shit*house' — it didn't look recently done either, but no one had bothered to fix it.

"Are you ready for some fun with a capital F!?" his dad shouted, clapping his hands together.

"Can't we go somewhere else? Like... I don't know... *home*?"

Markus's smile flickered again.

"Come on. It'll be fun"—his dad ran to the entrance—"I promise." Then he disappeared into the gloom beyond.

Christopher took a single step forward.

Then stopped.

Christopher turned and walked to the nearest bin, throwing away the rest of his pizza, before heading back to the carnival's entrance.

He would never have left if he'd known that that day would be the last time he'd see his father.

* * * * *

Cassandra and Christopher walked down the hill. Below them, smoke and fire and the occasional explosion lit up the night's darkness. The carnival seemed to be contained inside a seemingly endless fence. No, not fence, just rows of giant stakes. Christopher swallowed hard. He wanted nothing more than to turn around. But where would he even go?

The hill led down to a wide plateau where the Carnival was set up. Cassandra led them around the fence of stakes, to a single white booth. Red paint dribbled down the sides even as Christopher watched. It bubbled occasionally, and steam wafted out from it into the night.

The man inside the compartment wore a top hat and a disinterested look. He had a neat mustache that he was carefully running a miniature comb through. Behind him was a clock. It was exactly midnight.

"Mm?" hummed the top-hatted man, as they approached the open window.

"We want to speak to The Fool," said Cassandra, her voice firm.

"Well, little lass, we all want things we can't have," replied the man, flicking his mustache out at them. "I *want* a vacation in Arcadia with a blonde woman who has the most massive-"

"I don't think I made myself clear. I *need* to speak to The Fool. I think there's been a mistake."

"I *need* to see your tickets," he replied, nonchalant.

"I am the daughter of Death. I do not *need* a ticket," said Cassandra, her eyes starting to smolder once again. "You know that, Rufus."

"Aye. But the lad there certainly does. No mortal gets into the The Carnival of Night without a ticket."

18

Cassandra let out a frustrated groan before turning to Christopher. "Just show him your ticket."

"I- I don't have a t-"

"You don't..." She sighed. "Show him the *back of your head*."

"Oh," said Christopher, turning around. "Well how was I to know that! This is my first time being dead. And to be honest, I think I'm doing a pretty damn good job of it."

Cassandra smiled. "Yes, okay. Sorry."

"Closer," said Rufus. "Step back again. Closer. There's a good lad. Right, let's see what we've got here." Rufus picked up a tiny flashlight from his table, clicked it, and shone it into the wound. "Oh yes. Mmm hmm. Mmm hmm," he mumbled, as he inspected the cavern. "Oh yes. *Definitely in the right place.* And what good timing! I heard there's a job opening on Pitfall, you lucky fella."

"He's not here for a job. He won't be here for long at all."

"Pitfall?"

"Don't ask," said Cassandra.

"Oh, it's a hell of a ride," chuckled Rufus as he began to wind a lever in front of him. With a repetitive *clunk*, four of the wooden stakes began to lower into the ground. "But it takes a lot of maintenance."

"Where can we find The Fool?" Cassandra asked.

Rufus glanced at the clock behind him. It was still at exactly midnight.

"Mmm, at this time? Best bet's the funhouse."

The familiar feeling of dread began to unfurl itself in Christopher's stomach.

CHAPTER FIVE

A stream of heat erupted in front of Christopher's face, forcing him to step back. His skin felt on fire as he turned to see a scrawny man — little more than skin stapled to bones — blowing a plume of deep red out of his mouth. It lasted maybe three or four seconds, then the fire seemed to get sucked back into the man; his adam's apple rocked as he swallowed the flames into his stomach.

Christopher watched open-mouthed as the man turned and locked eyes with him. His lips were black and cracked, and his face was terribly warped. It was like looking at a once fine painting of a man, that had since been ruined by water getting onto it — the paint had leaked and run, distorting the brush strokes and creating something entirely new. Entirely dreadful.

A hand tugged on his shoulder. "Come on," said Cassandra, pulling him onward as another burst of flame exploded out behind, ravaging the spot he had been standing on a few seconds before.

"This is just... *purgatory?*" Christopher asked.

"That's one name for it. But The Fool doesn't like people using it here... you're much better off saying *The Carnival*." Cassandra lifted her hands and made air quotes, "The party that truly never ends."

"Has it always existed, then? The Carnival."

"Yes. Well, at least in a way. What I mean is, it's not always been like this. It changes, as you mortals and your lives and imaginations change. Like, back when Bacchus was Lord of the Between, a wagon would have taken you here, and this place was more, uh..." Cassandra paused and considered her next word carefully.

"More?"

"*Orgiastic.*"

Christopher raised his eyebrows. "That doesn't sounds so terrible. In fact, it sounds… *kind of great.*"

Cassandra let out a puff of air. "Yeah. I'm sure you'd know."

"Well, I-" He felt his cheeks grow warm.

"I don't mean it was just full of people having sex. That's missing the point. *Anyway*, it's been The Fool's Carnival for as long as most here care to remember. *The Carnival of Night*, as he christened it."

As they snaked their way through the carnival, Christopher glanced continually from one side to the other, from one bizarre sight to another. On his right, a red and white Helter-skelter towered high into the dark sky. On his left was — what he first thought — a coconut shy, with a half dozen people throwing spiked balls at the targets, attempting to knock them off their stands. As they neared it he realized, swallowing back disgust, that the targets weren't coconuts, but severed heads.

"Holy shi-" he gasped, his words dying in his throat as the eyes on one of the faces flicked open.

Its mouth began to move.

"*Helpppp mee-*"

A half second later, in a red splattering, a ball flew into the face knocking it clean off its perch. There was a tremendous cheer from the gathered crowd.

"**Ding, ding!**" cried a hugely obese man from behind the stall, as he bent down and picked the fallen head up by its hair. "We have a winner! We have a winner! Here's your ticket, ma'am, please take it to the prize stall and exchange it for whatever there you desire." The man twisted the head down onto a tiny stake, skewering it back into position. The eyes were closed again and it looked lifeless, except for the blood still trickling down its cheeks.

"This place... is... just... " Christopher couldn't finish his sentence.

"I know. *I know*. But it could be worse. Trust me."

"That doesn't make me feel much better."

"You'll be fine. We won't be here long."

"You mentioned someone called Bacc- *Baccuss?*"

"*Bacchus*"

"Yeah. Bacchus. The name rings a bell. Who's he?"

"The previous Lord of the Between, before The Fool. He was okay apparently — not that I ever met him. He was a lesser deity. The Greeks worshiped him as Dionysus, and then the Romans as Bacchus, which he preferred, but he was Lord of the Between for a long time before either."

"So, what happened to him?"

"Who knows! One day he was just... *not here*, and the next night, The Fool appears. It's been night time at The Fool's Carnival ever since."

"And *The Fool*, he's also one of these *lesser deities*?"

"I don't know much about him. No one does. Not where he came from or who he is. But lesser deity... hm, I'm not so sure about that. I know for certain that he's powerful, and he's the prime suspect for Bacchus's vanishing. Not that the Council of Gods could find any evidence."

Christopher let out a breath. "The *Council?* There's a council!? Don't they care about what The Fool's doing here? How he's running it. This place looks like Hell, at least to me it does."

"It's complicated. It *has* gotten worse here though, that I'll admit. It seems to get worse every time I visit. But as long as The Carnival still runs then, *no*, no one really cares. And besides, like I said, The Fool is *powerful*. Who's going to challenge him? I suspect it's why the Council left it well enough alone. Look, all you need to know is that he's the master of this place, and his word is... well, it's the *final* word."

"*Who's going to challenge him*? Uh gee, well let me see... How about... *you?* I mean I saw what you did to the creature on the hill and-"

Cassandra laughed. "*Me?* Are you serious? I have a *little* connection to the Gods, but really, I'm a fragment-deity. My father gave a slither of himself for me to exist. Think of me as a magician at a kids party — to those who don't know any better, sure, I look impressive. But to those who do know how the tricks are done..."

"Then I guess I'm one of those kids staring up at you and going *oooh* and *aaah*."

Cassandra smiled. "Yes, I suppose you are. Okay, we're almost there."

The funhouse flashed manically in the distance, its many bulbs gleaming through the darkness like the eyes of a demon spider. *Come,* it seemed to say. *I'm waiting for you, Christopher. Come into my web.*

There was no clown juggling in front of it this time, but all the same it brought back the uneasiness he'd felt long ago. The guilt in his gut that had invaded him on the day he'd heard his father's plane had crashed. The guilt that had never really left him but instead lay dormant, waiting to rear its ugly head whenever anything good happened to him. Whenever there was a chance of happiness.

"I want you to wait outside," Cassandra said. "At least, for a few minutes. I'll come get you when we're ready."

"Can't I come with you?"

"I think it's better I speak with The Fool first. *Alone*. Do me a favor and don't move one step from here. You don't want to end up like one of those heads back there. Okay?"

Christopher nodded as Cassandra disappeared into the dark portal.

He leaned back against the cold metal of the funhouse and took long, slow breaths. *It's going to be okay*, he repeated. *It's all okay. Going to be fine. It's just a carnival. You used to like them.*

A burst of high-pitched mechanical laughter rang out from somewhere inside the funhouse. It forced a shiver down Christopher's spine and sprinkled goosebumps in its wake.

Two women walked past him — one with a gaping hole running clean through her cheek. Their eyes locked on him, their mouths moving as they gossiped to one another a little too quietly for him to hear. He thought maybe he heard, "*Moving on soon,*" but he wasn't certain.

Another minute or so passed. He tried to breathe through his mouth to help block out The Carnival's stench — but even so, he could taste on his throat the bitterness of petrol and smoke, and a disgusting stink of singed hair.

A scream ripped through the atmosphere of the night as if it were a knife blade. For a second, he thought the voice belonged to Cassandra. His entire body tensed up, but he swallowed hard and readied himself to enter the funhouse.

You can do this, Christopher. You owe her.

He had taken only a single step inside, when the scream came again.

It wasn't coming from within, after all.

It was coming from behind him.

CHAPTER SIX

Christopher turned to see a distant circle of men, women, and what looked like a few young children. They were shouting and baying and raising their arms at something within their ranks. The scream he'd heard had to have come from inside that circle. And it hadn't been a scream of pleasure or excitement, but of *fear*.

Of dread.

"I'll be right back, Cassandra," he whispered into the funhouse's entrance, before sprinting towards the circle. His legs were heavy, unhappy at moving, and *especially* unhappy about where they were moving to.

"Dance, wench," a deep voice boomed, "Dance 'till ya drop!"

Laughter from the crowd.

"This is what happens when you don't obey the rules of the fare."

Christopher pushed his way through the wave of people as popcorn and drink rained down upon him. "Excuse me," he said — not that anyone either noticed, cared or excused him. "Excuse me!" He weaved his way through the throng of bodies until finally, he was at the front of the circle.

"*Oh God...*"

Inside the wall of people, the ground was littered with burning coal, bright-red and smoldering fiercely. On the coals, stood a middle-aged woman with long brown hair and a terrified expression plastered across her face.

There was no skin on her feet. No muscle or tendons. There was just... *bone*.

It wasn't until her ankles that patches of blackened skin began to smatter her legs.

"Dance!" came the voice again, deep and threatening. It came from a huge, barrel chested man standing on the other side of the circle. Dribble ran down his many chins and his smile made Christopher want to vomit. He wore a blood-stained apron that fell to his knees and fluttered up and down excitedly in the breeze.

The woman on the coals tried to turn, as if attempting to perform a mockery of a pirouette — but her feet were not as willing as her body, and she fell onto the coals. Her hands hit first; she let out an agonized scream as they sizzled in a gush of smoke.

More laughter.

"Back to your feet, woman!" said the man. "You ain't done yet. Not by a long shot."

Christopher didn't mean to say *anything*, but the yell burst out of him as if he were an overfilled balloon that had just been pricked.

"Leave her alone!"

It only took a second for a hush to fall over the crowd. A blanket of utter silence. Even the usual blaring background music seemed to have stopped to watch what happened next.

Many eyes fell upon him. The entire crowd inspecting the idiot who had spoken up.

"What the *fuck* did you just say, lad?" It was the huge aproned man who was staring at him, his head cocked.

"I said"—Christopher swallowed—"leave her *alone*." His voice sounded wispy and weak in comparison to the man's. But he had to act strong now. If he showed any weakness... He took a deep breath, "What's the matter, are you deaf as well as ugly?"

Hints of stifled laughter haunted the air around him.

"I thought that's what you said," replied the massive man as he strode onto the coals. "I was hoping it was, at least." His feet were bare, yet he didn't so much as flinch as coal crunched beneath him. He placed a hand into a pocket on the front of his apron and fished around.

"I'm going to introduce you to my friend Cleave. You two are about to become very well acquainted."

He pulled out a long, gleaming butcher's knife and held it tight in his hand.

"*Why did you have to piss off Chef?*" whispered the man next to him as he stepped away. Christopher realized the entire crowd was backing off, quietly dispersing into the night to watch from the safety of the shadows.

The woman who had been dancing on the coals glanced at him, then crawled on her hands and knees over the burning rocks, and into the darkness beyond.

"I need something for tonight's soup," said Chef. "And you look just the thing." A green tongue flicked out of his mouth and left a covering of saliva dripping down around his lips.

Christopher stepped back as Chef drew closer.

"Oh, no point running boy," said Chef as he took in a long breath through his nose. "I will smell your stink where ever you might go. That you can be sure of."

"You're - you're sick in the head," was all Christopher could manage as he blinked back tears of fear.

Chef's wicked smile grew, his lips curling devilishly. "Compliment's will get you no where. *Complements*, they'll help you more. Soon."

Christopher could smell the man now. The stench of rotting meet reeked from his pores. He took another step back — he

27

didn't see the log waiting behind him. His head thumped against the ground and his body went weak.

The man now hovered over him, his eyes wide. "I'm going to enjoy carving you up, boy," he said, as he raised his knife above his head. "You'll enjoy this place far more as a thousand little pieces being shitted out here there and every-fucking-where."

Christopher instinctively covered his head with his arms. He thought of his mom. His dad.

A gunshot rang out — a deafening boom that made Christopher's ears sting. The butcher's knife clattered to the ground next to him. There was a scream, muffled mostly by the ringing in his ears. He moved his arms away from his face to see Chef; the man's arm was still up in the air, but his index finger was... *gone*. Blood fountained out of the wounded stub.

"I will stew you for this!" yelled Chef at *someone* behind Christopher. Chef staggered forward towards the figure. "You hear me?"

"If you could make a stew at all, I'd be impressed. Hell, if you could boil water, that would be something. But either way, you're going to want all your fingers to try," said the voice. Calm and relaxed. "And Pearl seems to have other plans for you."

Christopher and Chef noticed the skinny dog at the same time, as it gnawed happily on the fallen appendage.

"Give me that back, you little rat bastard!" yelled chef, stooping down and making a grab for the dog. But the animal was too agile for him and rolled easily out of the way. It looked up at Chef, growled protectively, then ran off deep into the Carnival.

Chef glanced one last time at the figure, before chasing after his quickly escaping finger.

Christopher's head was spinning and he felt nauseous.

CHAPTER SEVEN

Death took in the morning's pile of paperwork, that sat like a fluttering white mountain on his desk, before allowing himself a languorous sigh. He sank back into his seat. It had been such a long night's work, and now — in almost no time at all — the paperwork had once again accumulated. Too many humans, that was the problem these days. He used to pay them each a little bit of attention, when he collected them. Had a bit of fun. Sometimes, he would even *get to know them*. Now, they were just names on a list that needed to be signed off before they could be collected.

Why was his tie so damn tight this morning? Maybe he would start wearing a cloak again. But he did *like* suits. They looked smart. Professional. Times had changed and so had he.

He loosened the knot, undid the top button on his shirt and grabbed his coffee. "One step at a time," he said, as he brought the steaming beverage close to his nose. "Ahh."

Death wasn't yet in the mood to stand, so instead he tugged out a random piece of paper from low on the stack. The tower wobbled nervously as Death laid the lucky page down on his desk.

There was a knock on his door.

"Enter," Death said, grateful for the interruption.

His assistant stepped in, his usual sheepish expression looking somehow *more* sheepish today.

"Yes, Edward?"

"I've, erm, I've got a scroll for you, sir."

"Well add it to the pile," Death mumbled. "I'll get there... *sooner or later.*"

"Sir, it's special delivery."

"Oh?"

"From The Carnival."

"The Carnival..." Death repeated. Was that what they were calling purgatory these days? Yes, that was it. Purgatory. And purgatory was his daughter's job, not his. She seemed to be getting on well with it, too. At least, he'd not *heard* any complaints. "Send it through to my daughter," he instructed. "The Carnival is not my concern."

Edward stared at his nervously shuffling feet.

"But that's just it, sir. It's... it's about *Cassandra.*"

CHAPTER EIGHT

"Just stay seated," said the man. "I'll fix you a drink."

Christopher heard a *pop*, then the sound of liquid sloshing into a cup. He looked around him: he was sitting in a rocking chair outside an ancient trailer, its once-white paint chipped and its metal rusting. A little distance away, on Christopher's right sat a boarded up stall with a sign above it that read '*Duck Shot*'.

The man pushed a mug into his hand. "Drink it slowly. It's a little strong, but it'll make you feel a lot better."

"Who are you?" Christopher asked. The man looked like something out of one of those ancient cowboy movies. He had high boots, a tan leather waistcoat, and an old cloak thrown carelessly over his shoulders. On his head was a brown wide-brimmed hat, and tied around his face, covering his mouth and flowing over his throat, was a red handkerchief.

If not a cowboy, an outlaw.

"You can call me Derek."

"Are you... are you like, a law-man here?"

Derek let out a mock laugh. "There ain't much law here. Just the word."

"Were you a cowboy? Before, you know." Christopher sipped at his mug; he coughed and spluttered as the liquid singed his throat. "What—ugh—what is this!?"

"I said drink slow. Before I died? Nope, I was never no cowboy. Heck, we didn't even have cowboys back in my day.

But times change, and a fisherman — which is what I *was*, incidentally — might have been suitable for a game of hook-a-fish, but no one wants to play that kind of thing any more. So I moved on, and well, this is my new role. *Partner*," he added, in a shoddy accent.

Christopher glanced over at the Duck Shot stall again. "So that's yours then," he asked, nodding toward it.

"Yep. I made it, I run it," he answered proudly. "Now, I think that's enough questions from you to me, for the moment at least. You're new here, right? So why don't *you* tell *me* what the heck you were doi-"

"Are we all having a g-g-good night?!" came a voice drifting from afar, and that yet somehow surrounded them totally.

A cheer ran out from all over The Carnival, as if answering the call.

"Ah, *shit*," said Derek.

"What is it?"

"Can you walk?"

"I think so."

"Mmm. Well, best follow me."

Christopher jumped off his seat followed the faux-cowboy as they meandered through The Carnival. It didn't take long for the lights of the funhouse to catch Christopher's attention.

"I said, are we all having f-f-fun?" repeated a slim, costumed figure standing outside the funhouse. He wore a single piece of clothing that covered him entirely. Two stripes ran up it from toe to head, one black the other white. On his face was a cream mask, like one of those Guy Fawkes ones, Christopher thought, but with a long twisted beak where its nose should be, the tip of which was bright red.

There was another cheer. Louder and full of enthusiasm. Too much enthusiasm, he thought.

"That's more like it!" yelled the figure. Only, Christopher realized it *wasn't* the figure that was speaking. It was a *skull* that he held in his right hand, painted bright reds and greens that pulsed vividly in the darkness. It wouldn't look out of place at that Mexican festival of the dead, he thought.

Its teeth lifted and chattered in a satisfied stutter. **"G-g-g-great to hear! Because it's just turned midnight and the p-p-party is only now getting started!"**

"Is that..."

"*Yes,*" said Derek.

If that's The Fool, Christopher wondered, *where was Cassandra?*

He didn't have long to dwell on it, as he noticed The Fool's hand twisting slowly, the skull it held turning with it.

Turning.

Turning.

Until finally, as its teeth clattered once more, it settled on Christopher.

CHAPTER NINE

"S-s-step forward, boy."

Christopher remained perfectly still. Perhaps The Fool was talking to someone else in the crowd. Someone behind him. But he knew deep down that the skull was staring at him, and him alone.

"I said"—The Fool's voice dropped to a whisper that hissed seductively in Christopher's ears—"S-s-step forward, boy." He could feel the words travel down his spine like fingertips tapping.

Christopher wanted desperately to resist, but his body obeyed the instruction without his mind's consent. He so wanted to fight the impulse that had burrowed into his brain and taken control, but it was irresistible. He paced slowly forward until stopping a foot or so away from the skull-cradling figure.

"Good boy," crooned The Fool, as he began circling Christopher like a shark sniffing a bleeding body. But instead of going in for the kill, he lifted and tilted the skull around him, as if it was inspecting him. The paint on the skull seemed fresh, the coat of vivid colors not just glossy, but *flowing*. Undulating as it changed patterns, the white and green highlights trickling into new designs around the eyes and cheeks.

He felt like the skull was peering into his soul. And it made him feel... *pleased*. A feeling of warmth was growing in his stomach, and suddenly, bizarrely, he never wanted to leave The

Carnival. And beyond that, like nothing he'd ever desired before, he wanted to make The Fool happy.

The skull came to rest in front of Christopher's face, and his eyes locked onto the dark, empty sockets. No, not just dark, but a blackness so far beyond the abyss that he thought, for a second, he could see a light.

"*I've been waiting for you, Christopher.*"

"I am here to serve you." Had he just said that? The voice has been his, but surely...

"You've already served me more than y-y-you know."

"I am pleased to have done so, my lord."

"Are you enjoying my little Carnival?"

"Yes. Immensely. I feel fulfille-"

A light-bulb flickered somewhere in front of him — red to yellow to nothing. He glanced over to a dead light that was sitting just above the door to the funhouse. The funhouse... *Cassandra*... The grip of the trespasser in his mind lessened momentarily.

"Where is she?" he rasped.

"P-p-pardon?" inquired the Fool, the skull violently pulling away from his face, its voice sharp and tinged with annoyance. "What did you say?"

"Cassandra. *Where is she?*" Christopher's voice was firm now. Demanding.

"Ahh, the D-D-Death child."

"Yes."

"She has gone. G-g-gone back home to her realm and to her duties."

"*What?*" Christopher's heart plummeted to his shoes. "You're lying! She can't be gone — she wouldn't have just left me."

"She came to me for her payment, and then w-w-went."

35

"Payment?"

"To deliver you. To me."

"She was supposed to... she promised she would help me get out of here."

"*Ahahahaha*" The skull's teeth chattered as it laughed. "Mortals don't leave The Carnival, C-C-Christopher. *Ever.* She knew that. Oh, you look so very disappointed. If it is any consolation, she looked for you before she left, to say goodbye, I presume. She exited the funhouse with me, and her little face fell m-m-most adorably as she looked around for you."

"I..." He swallowed back a mix of tears and memories of years before.

"I think she'd hoped you'd follow her in." The Fool took his free hand to the skull and pretended to wipe away tears from under the empty eye sockets. "Boo hoo hoo!" His voice suddenly became sing-song and the skulls jaw widened into a type of grin. "Now- now the real question: where, *oh where*, should a boy like you work? The P-P-Pit, p-p-perhaps? It'll help get you *adjusted.* Down in the Pit, where the creatures crunch and crack. A nice little place for a nice little lad."

"Why did you want me here? Why pay Cassandra to deliver *me*?"

"All in g-g-good time. Now, let's get you to the Pit-"

"Excuse me, partner."

Christopher looked up to see Derek walking across to them. The usual swagger in his gait was gone, but his voice was still as calm as ever.

"What is it, fisherman?" asked The Fool, a tinge of annoyance diluting his voice once more.

"Just that, well gee, I could do with a new assistant on my stall. Caroline hasn't been the same since you made her ride the Helter-Skelter, and I very much need someone to cover me on my breaks."

36

The skull grimaced. "Are b-b-breaks still a thing? Ahhh! *Very well.* It matters not where he works right now. He can help you, *temp-p-porarily.*"

"Thank you, sir. That's most kind."

"After all, we'll be moving on soon anyway." The Fool raised his arm high above his head. **Did you all hear me? Shortly, The Carnival will be moving to pastures green and new! And we're going to be expanding ex-ex-ex-exponentially.**"

There was a mix of cheers and confused voices in the air around them: *Moving? Where to? The Carnival never moves!*

The Fool lowered his arm so that the painted skull stared again at Christopher. "But not *quite* yet. I'm w-w-waiting for a guest to arrive first. Yes, you will help the fisherman until we are ready to leave.

Derek placed a hand on Christopher's back, pushing him gently away from The Fool.

"Work on your accent, f-f-fisherman," the skull screeched out after them. "You make a dismal cowboy. And remember b-b-boy: to the wise, life is a problem; to the fool, a solution!"

There was a trail of frivolous laughter in the air as they walked back towards Derek's trailer.

* * * * *

The walk was mostly wordless. Christopher was full of questions, slithering around his brain, turning and twisting and never making any sense. Most of them had to do with Cassandra. A girl he hardly knew, and yet felt like he *knew* better than nearly anyone else. He was wrong about that, he supposed. And then... there was the question of how he was going to get out of this place alone.

"You okay?"

"Huh?" Christopher replied nonsensically.

"Yeah, you're okay. Say, how did you do that back there?"

"Do what?"

"Resist him. I've not seen anyone do that."

"Resist?"

"Yeah. When he was talking to you — you didn't just say what he was making you, did you? You asked about that Death child instead. How'd you do it?"

"Oh. Cassandra." He shrugged. "I don't know. I just... *did.*"

Derek grunted. "Whatever you say."

Christopher nodded.

"You look anxious. *Relax.* You'll get used to The Carnival. Eventually."

"I don't want to get 'used to it'. I don't belong here."

"You must have done *something* to earn your ticket."

"I didn't."

"I figure you did and you just don't remember. Memories like that, they hide like a ship behind the ocean fog. But eventually, the mist lifts and the boat is just left bobbing there, clear and empty, and alone with its sins."

"... What does your ship look like?"

Derek bit down on his tongue. "Mine... mine looks like two empty bottles and three tiny graves." He didn't say any more, but his pale face — what Christopher could see of it behind the handkerchief — had turned as hard as marble. Christopher thought it best not to pursue the enquiry.

By the time the Duck Shot stall came into view, Christopher could make out a queue of a dozen or so people lazily lined outside it, like a snake whose body didn't quite connect.

"Customers?" he asked.

Derek let out laugh as they reached the stall. "*Ducks.* They, my new assistant, are tonight's ducks."

Christopher looked up at Derek and frowned. "Ducks?"

"You'll see soon enough."

"Did you really need a new assistant?"

Derek shrugged. "Can't hurt to have one."

Christopher nodded. "Is the Pit as bad as it sounded?"

"Can be. Most of the time, worse."

"Then, thank you."

Derek looked at him. His face softened, and Christopher wondered if behind the handkerchief there might be something of a smile.

"You're welcome. Now, let's get this place open for business." Derek turned to address the queue of bodies, raising his hands in apology. "Won't keep you waiting much longer, folks! My new assistant here will get you ready for your night." He looked back at Christopher. "Follow me."

As they walked around the stall Christopher began to get an appreciation for how large the boarded up structure really was. It must have been three or four times the size of a regular old duck shooting stall. They arrived at a wooden door at the rear of the structure with the words: 'staff only' sloshed across it in broad white paint strokes.

Derek lifted a chain from off his neck that had a key dangling on its end and turned it in the lock. "Wait here," he instructed Christopher as he walked inside. He returned a moment later with a dozen yellow rubber ducks cradled in his arms. Each duck had a black strap on its belly. "Here," he said, dumping them into Christopher's arms. "The people back there — put one on each of their heads. Nice and tight."

"*What*? Why would I-"

"I told you, *they're our ducks today*. Now get to it while I open the shutters and check the rifles."

Christopher walked back to the queue of people. As they saw him, they fell to their knees, bowing their heads to the ground. For a second, he thought they were worshiping him... then he realized they were waiting for the ducks to be strapped on.

They didn't talk to him as he got them ready. Didn't reply to his questions — didn't even make eye contact. He wondered who they were, or why they'd been chosen. He had so many questions he needed to ask Derek.

But the biggest question, the one that burned in his mind like a white-dwarf, was about Cassandra.

He glanced in the direction of the funhouse.

Why was it still calling to him?

What was waiting for him in there?

CHAPTER TEN

Death looked at the scroll again.

You had such a pretty daughter - so sweet and innocent.

Now I have such a pretty girl. Less sweet and innocent.

And in fact, much less pretty :(

:)

"Sir?" said Edward, his voice as shaky as his hands. "Is there anything I can do?"

Death scrunched the scroll up in his fist, then looked up at his assistant. He tried to keep his voice calm and level. "I have to pop out of the office for a time. Be so good as to fetch me my scythe."

CHAPTER ELEVEN

HOWDY PARTNER! WELCOME TO DUCK SHOT!

Rules of the Game

Twelve ducks are swimming in the pond — but these aren't your regular old country ducks, no siree, these naughty ducks have been misbehaving and eating all the farmer's corn! Now he doesn't have enough stored up to feed his family this winter! :(

*Can **you** help the poor farmer avenge his soon-to-starve-to-death family?*

You will be awarded one (1) point for a clean hit on any single duck. You will be awarded five (5) points for hitting the head of a swimmer as they pop up from beneath the water for a lungful of air.

One (1) token gets you six (6) rifle rounds. Fifteen (15) points are needed for a prize booth ticket.

Good luck, partner! Yee-haw!

Terms and Conditions

If you hit a swimmer whilst they are submerged, then gee, bad news compadre — you have instantly lost.

Have fun!

By hitting a submerged swimmer, you waiver, reject, and repudiate your right to a full corporeal existence and agree to be our replacement duck during the following night's festivities.

If Nurse can stitch you back together after, she will. But Nurse makes no promises!

By partaking in any game at all at The Carnival, you have agreed to grant The Fool full ownership of your soul.

All hail The Fool :)

* * * * *

It wasn't the boom of the rifle that made Christopher turn away from the chalk-scrawled rule board — he had already gotten somewhat used to gunfire and barely even flinched now — but it was the gurgled scream coming from the red water behind him.

"Ahahaha, you got 'im, you go 'im! What a shot Memphis, honey — *what a shot!*" exclaimed a grinning pale-faced lady, as she slapped a hand against the shooter's back.

"Just need one more of those bastards, and I'll be getting you something good tonight, my love."

"Get that one again, Memph! Look at it go — have you ever seen that many bubbles? It'll be coming back up any second now!"

The wounded man was still wailing beneath the water, the duck on his head skimming about like a plane in its death throws as it bounced against the ground. Red fuel trailed above his head, blossoming out in the murky water.

That was the swimmer's third bullet taken tonight, and Christopher had felt terrible each and every time. Derek had tried to assure him the ducks would be fine and that this was one of the more *humane*games at The Carnival. He liked Derek, but humane was not a word he'd use for Duck Shot.

"Oh I will, babycakes," said Memphis, taking aim again. He began tracing the line of the frantic duck with the rifle.

"Doesn't count, compadre," said Derek.

"Excuse me, runt?" said Memphis, not taking his eye off the duck.

"Your shot. It doesn't count. He was below the water. *It was a bad shot*. You needed to wait for him to rise."

"**Bad shot?**" the man growled.

"Are you going to take that shit from him, Memph?"

Christopher's body tensed, sensing the inevitable escalation.

"*He came up for air*. He was *clearly* above the water!" spat Memphis. "Not my fault you're blind. Now, I got two more shots and I need-"

"No more shots. I'm tagging you for tomorrow night's game."

"Like fuck you are!" yelled Memphis, turning his rifle on Derek.

Derek's hands dropped to the holstered pistols on his waist.

"*Try me.*"

Memphis's finger pressed against the trigger — but before he could squeeze it, two shots rang out and a spray of red mist exploded about him. Both bullets had struck him in the centre of his forehead.

For a brief second, the man staggered forward, gun still aimed at Derek. Then dribble crawled out of his mouth, the gun fell, and he collapsed to his knees.

"You lose, compadre," said Derek, re-holstering his weapons and striding across to the freshly lobotomised man.

"Son of a bitch," screeched the woman as she snatched the rifle up from the floor.

Christopher impulsively grabbed a metal pole resting against the wall next to him, meant for fishing out loose ducks from the water. He brought it down with a tremendous *clank* onto the woman's head. His hands and arms rang and he imagined for a second that this must be how a church bell feels on Sundays.

The lady collapsed next to Memphis.

Derek glanced up at him. "I had the situation under control."

"Oh... I thought maybe you hadn't seen and-"

"But uh, I appreciate it. Good to have a second pair of eyes and all that."

"Right." Christopher took a deep breath as he tried to hide the nerves that clung to his every muscle.

"Hey... he *was* below the water, right?"

"...I didn't see. Sorry." He glanced down at the bodies. "I sure as hell hope so, though!"

Derek shrugged. "He was. I'm pretty sure. Well, that's four for tomorrow, so far."

As the ringing in Christopher's ears from the gunshots died down, the usual carnival music drifted back in. He peered out across the night in the direction of the funhouse.

"Do you mind if I take ten? I could do with a stroll."

Derek was dragging the man's body around to the side of the Duck Shot; he lugged it on top of two other still twitching half-people.

"*Already need a break?*"

"I won't be long."

"Mm. Guess I can handle it alone. Have most nights, anyway."

"Thanks," he replied, already walking away. "Be back soon."

"Be careful!"

* * * * *

Christopher watched the funhouse from the relative safety of distant shadows, not really sure what he expected to see. But no one came in. No one came out. The door was decorated to look like a clown's mouth with thick grinning lips painted above it, and a wide red step below to match. Bulbs flashed like colorful

45

cameras around it, radiating an eerie light on the outside of the building, but making the pitch black of the mouth itself look all the more conspicuous.

He looked around — no one seemed to be watching him — and skulked towards the door.

"Come on. It'll be fun. I promise."

His father's words echoed inside his head; his hands scrunched into balls as he stepped over the lip.

Blackness.

Total, engulfing blackness.

Somehow it even blocked out the view of The Carnival behind him, as if his face had been wrapped in a blanket.

A shrill laugh rang out behind him and he jumped back, goosebumps prickling his skin. He waited, panting and unmoving, for The Fool to grab him and drag him to the Pit — or somewhere worse. *But it hadn't been the fool, had it?* It had been that same mechanical laughter he'd heard while waiting outside the funhouse for Cassandra.

With a deep breath, he took a step forward. Then another. And another. His shoes clanked loudly against what must have been metal beneath him.

Another sound.

A noise like rising thunder greedily engulfed the passageway — then the first heralding ripple of the oncoming metal tsunami ran beneath him. He wobbled, staggering back as the floor itself moved, but somehow — *somehow* — he kept his balance. But he couldn't keep it for long, as the ripples turned into violent waves, throwing him off his feet and hard onto the ground.

With a grunt, he forced himself up to his knees, but the dark waves struck again, sending him sprawling backwards.

He cursed as he scrambled to his knees once more, looking desperately about him for the exit.

But only darkness.

He was trapped.

Another wave sent him rolling and ricocheting down the hallway, slamming against an unseen wall and leaving him feeling like a marble in a children's game. He wasn't sure if his head was spinning, or if it was the hall.

He let out a frustrated scream. "You can do this, Chris! You don't even *want* to find the exit — you want to go on. Come on, get it together. Be brave for once in your life!"

He rolled over onto his belly and began to crawl forward into the darkness. The floor twisted and shook beneath him as if trying to flick him off it, but he slithered and scrabbled against it, slowly moving onward.

He let out a relieved laugh. "That all you got?!"

As if trying to meet the challenge, the floor rocked and jerked beneath him like a rodeo bull. Christopher's chin smacked metal and his teeth bit deep into his tongue. The familiar taste of blood flooded his mouth, but he kept on creeping forward.

Eventually, he saw *something* in the distance.

A bleak light.

"Come on. Almost there. Almost there."

He edged ever closer to the light.

There was a room beyond, he was sure of it, and there was something tall and silver in there. No, not just one *something* — lots of them.

The waves beneath began to die, falling back to gentle ripples; he clambered to his feet and crept forward with his back and legs bent, ready for another assault.

Yes, there was definitely *something* ahead.

Something moving.

For a moment, he thought it was his own reflection in the many mirrors that decorated the room beyond.

Then he realised what it was.

"Cassandra?"

CHAPTER TWELVE

"Y-you'll need a ticket," said the man in the booth. "I can't let you into The Carnival without a ticket."

Death turned to Rufus, his eyes — even his pupils — a wicked white. He clutched his scythe tight in his right hand.

"I'm sorry, but Fool's rules." Rufus gingerly ran a comb through his moustache. "And well, ain't nothing I can do about that. I'm sure you understand. Now, if you could please move out of the way in case any*actual* ticket holders arrive..."

Death took a step towards the booth. Rufus yelped and pushed himself back against his chair. "Please stay away from the booth, sir!" He pointed a finger frantically at a sign stuck onto the glass window. "See? Rules are right there. Now take a step back, please!"

No touching the booth. No assaulting booth workers. No refunds. And -no- leaving! :)

Death's hand pressed against the brick of the booth's wall. A blue spark crackled under his skin.

Rufus gulped as the structure began to change. Withering and decaying as if decades were passing in seconds. The white and red brick was already crumbling. Paint fell off it as if it was skin flayed from a body, and dust snowed down onto Rufus's top-hat.

"You might wish to leave, now," said Death.

A brick fell next to Rufus's leg. He let out another yelp as he jumped off his chair and squirmed out of the booth's door. He fell to his knees outside, as a cloud of dust engulfed him, leaving him coughing and gagging. Behind him, the ticket booth collapsed with a roar into nothing more than a pile of indistinguishable rubble.

An icy hand grabbed the collar of his shirt and yanked him effortlessly to his feet. *Off* his feet.

"*Pl-*"—he wheezed and spluttered—"*Please, sir.*"

"Take me to The Fool," commanded Death, raising his scythe so that its tip rested an inch away from the man's nose. "Or your time in purgatory will have seemed like a joyride in heaven, compared to what I will do to you."

The man began to shake, his face pale.

"**N-n-no need for that**," came a chattering voice from behind.

CHAPTER THIRTEEN

Paddy turned the collar of his trench coat up in a vain effort to halt the rain's icy onslaught on his neck. The weather had been like this for weeks now — ever since Bacchus had abandoned them, in fact. It was as if the one God itself was weeping for the missing deity. Not that the one God actually cared enough for any of its children to *bother* shedding a tear. It had crept out the back door long ago, bored and disappointed by its own creations. Now the Heavens and Hells — and in-betweens, it seemed — were a mess of infighting Titans, half-Gods and lesser beings.

His tongue ran over his lips as the scent of cooked meats wafted over the various rides and found its way up his nostrils. How long had it been since he'd last eaten? His stomach was cramped and if he could have died of starvation, he figured he would have done so a long time before. How he missed the spit-roast pigs and the endlessly flowing wine! What he'd learned recently about purgatory was this: you don't appreciate anything when you think you have it forever. But once it's gone, it's *unbearable*.

Paddy trailed the smell of roasting juices past the Carousel, past the Ghost-house and Mine. All these rides the result of The Fool's re-branding. Modernisation. Even in death, you couldn't get away from it.

He sniffed the air and looked around.

There!

Up ahead, resting on a meat counter beneath a wide umbrella, was a huge rack of juice-dripping ribs, chopped and ready to eat. His hands ran instinctively into his thread bare pockets. No tokens, no coins — not even fluff. His stomach growled in annoyance.

He had to have them.

* * * * *

No one had seen him, he was pretty sure of that. He'd been stealthy and furtive, and now he was running into the shadows of the carousel with a huge rib cradled against his chest. He ran further — he wanted to be as far away from everyone as he could while he enjoyed his meal. The rides soon gave way to grey barked trees, dead or dying. He wriggled his way into the Forgotten Forest until he found a fallen log to sit on, where he could finally enjoy his juicy, illicit goods.

The rib was inches away from his drooling mouth when he heard the sound.

Water. Not falling water pattering on the canopy above, but *running water*.

He didn't remember there being a stream in the Forest...

Paddy took a single bite, tearing a mouthful of meat away from the bone, before getting to his feet and following the noise. Curiosity had been his downfall in life, and it wasn't going to lessen its grip on him now.

It was a constant roar by the time he found the sign standing outside the gloomy entrance:

~~TUNNEL OF LOVE~~. *OUT OF ORDER. DO NOT ENTER, BY ORDER OF THE FOOL :)*

Paddy frowned. How had he never heard of this ride? He'd explored the park thoroughly since the changes. *Hadn't he?*

Red eyed swans that looked as if they were nursing the mother of all hangovers lay on their sides by the edge of the water. It wouldn't have surprised him if the frothing rapids, churning and crashing against the edge, had thrown them onto the shore. It looked as unforgiving as an ocean on its very worst day.

Paddy walked tentatively along the edge of the canal, stopping cautiously every time a wave stretched a dripping arm out towards him. Before long, the river entered a tunnel where the sound of the waves became a deafening cacophony, its anger fully unleashed.

He felt uneasy. More than that. There was something very, *very,* wrong about this place. It was dim in the tunnel, not *quite* black, but almost. He wouldn't be able to see the waves coming for him now.

He was about to turn around and get the hell away from the ride, when he saw something shining in the water.

Two green emeralds.

They were submerged deep down in the water, shimmering and warped by the waves rolling across the surface, but... Had they just *blinked?*

He got to his knees and leaned over the edge, squinting into the watery abyss.

"Bacchus?"

"Oh dear," came a voice from behind, somehow cutting through the chaos of the waves. "First you take a rib, and then you stumble upon this. Oh dear, lad. Oh deary me. Fool won't like you seeing this. Not one little bit."

Paddy scrambled to his feet. His legs felt like over-cooked spaghetti and barely balanced him. "I didn't see-" He swallowed hard as light glinted off the cleaver.

"I hear the coconut stand is *recruiting* volunteers. Going to have to sew those pretty little lips up though." He licked his own lips with a long green tongue. "And I think there are going to be a few more ribs on the menu tonight."

"Ple-"

53

CHAPTER FOURTEEN

It *had* been Cassandra in the mirror's reflection. At least, it was Cassandra's still body that lay in the centre of the room, an almost surgical split running all the way down her open torso, as if Jack the Ripper had finally taken a sixth victim. Each mirror warped Cassandra's cadaver in its own dreadful way: stretching, shrinking, distorting or worse than any, gently swaying it as if she were still alive. Christopher thought of the blood tipped beak on The Fool's mask and a hate began to trickle through his veins, slowly diluting every inch of his body. A dreadful unforgiving malice.

He looked down at Cassandra again, and the hatred was swallowed by guilt. By sorrow and regret. Why hadn't he gone in with her? Not that he could have stopped The Fool... but still, there must have been *something* he could have done.

He sat down next to her and wept.

There was a *hiss* as smoke was released by some unseen tube, misting the room and momentarily hiding the mirrors. Christopher didn't notice.

He didn't notice either, at least for a moment, the ten tiny smudges on each of the mirrors that had appeared as the fog slowly lifted.

When he did see them, the hairs on his arms pricked up. He got to his feet and walked to a mirror that stretched his reflection out like it'd spent a night on a Rack.

Finger tips. That's what the smudges were. Small, but recognisable. They weren't there before... *were they?*

Then above the marks, the mirror began to gently mist. He wondered if he'd accidentally breathed on it... *But he hadn't.* He wasn't near enough to have done so. He glanced around him; *every mirror was fogged in exactly the same spot.*

Slowly, one by one, letters began to be formed, scrawled into the misty patches.

H E L P

He stood unmoving for a moment, not even daring to breath.

"*Cassandra?*" he whispered. "Is that you? Oh Jesus, please be you..."

The writing fogged over. A new message began.

HELLO, CHRISTOPHER.

More tears rolled down his face, scolding hot but desperately sweet in the corners of his mouth. "Oh, thank God!!" He palmed away the wetness from his eyes. "Thank God. *Cassandra*, how- how do I get you out of here? What do I do? Just tell me and I'll do it!"

It took a moment for the next message to begin.

I DON'T KNOW

"There must be a way. I'll break the mirrors!"

I'M NOT IN THEM

"...Well, what can I do? There must be something."

HE WANTS MY FATHER

"Who does? The Fool wants Death, you mean?"

YES

"... Why would he want your father?"

I DON'T KNOW

"Your father will destroy him. Right?"

The mirror fogged again, but not letters came.

55

"What do you want me to do, Cassandra?"

HE HAS A PART OF US

Christopher glanced down at Cassandra's open body. "Us? What, do you mean?"

A BONE. MY FATHER'S GIFT TO ME.

".. He has one of Death's bones? And... what, exactly do you want me to do? Do you mean I can bring you back with it!? Is that it, Cassandra?"

NO

Christopher's shoulders slumped. "Then, I don't understand. Can The Fool can use that in some way? Against your father?"

YES

"How?"

ANTIDOTE

For a moment, there was no word spoken nor written. Then, the mirror fogged again.

PLEASE HELP MY FATHER.

Christopher stepped towards the mirror. He pressed his finger tips gently against the smudge marks. "*I'm not leaving you here.*"

PLEASE

CHAPTER FIFTEEN

A bolt of flickering blue fire exploded out of Death's scythe. The Fool slammed into — and clean through — the wall of wooden stakes, his body travelling deep into The Carnival. There was the sound of bone crashing into metal. Of strained creaking.

Death stepped forward. He lifted a hand to the nearest stake, pressing his pale skin against it. The stake turned grey as it began to rot, as did the two that neighboured it. The rot spread rapidly, infecting the entire wall and quickly crumbling it to dust.

Death stepped over the ashen remnants and into The Carnival itself. He found the costumed body lying limp beneath the Ferris-wheel; the painted skull rested a foot or so away from the figure. A crowd gathered around them as carnival music blared loudly somewhere in the distance.

"I will ask you a last time. **Where is my daughter?**" Death's eyes smouldered, his white pupils turning to blazing rubies.

"Please. If you just g-g-give me a moment, I'll get her for you."

Death pulled his tie tight up to his neck. "You have exactly one minute."

The Fool's body crawled on all fours to the skull, then got to its feet, the bone head held in its right hand.

"Now, take me to my daughter," Death commanded.

The skull's mouth began to open. *Wider.* Wider still, as if it was a snake dislocating its jaw before swallowing a bison whole. The Fool placed his spare hand deep inside the mouth. There was a rattling inside the skull, before The Fool retracted his hand; something long and white was held tightly in its grasp.

Death swallowed. "Cassandra..." It took only a second for the despair he felt to turn into rage. He lifted his scythe in both hands high above his head.

"You are indeed a Fool!" he screamed as the sky clouded and white light exploded out of the metal tip; the bolt shot into The Fool's chest. "Now you will rot away into nothingness, and exist only as whispers for eternity!"

The Fool's back jerked and cracked. His knees bent and head twisted to the side. He let out a hideous pained scream.

"Ahhhhhh! Ahhhhhh! Ahhaaa ahahahahahaha! Ahahahahahaha! *You should see your face!*"

Death's mouth dropped as The Fool began to dance, jumping merrily between legs as he chuckled.

"That...can't..."

"Now, my turn, I b-b-believe."

A blizzard of creatures erupted from the skull's eye sockets and mouth. Locust, bot-flies, mosquitoes and a thousand other tiny creatures.

Death staggered back as he became host to a cloud of undulating black. There was a meek burst of blue light as he tried to disinfect himself, but they kept on biting and eating. *Why wouldn't they die?*

His skin, muscles, and sinews gave way to the ravenous horde. Death screamed as he collapsed to his knees.

By the time the creatures had finished feeding on him and flown away into the night, there was nothing left but a pile of clean white bones resting next to a scythe.

"B-b-bring me the Cage," The Fool instructed the two men now standing at his side.

* * * * *

Christopher stopped dead in his tracks when he saw the scene beneath the Ferris-wheel. A pile of bones was being scooped into what looked like a huge golden bird cage.

Next to it, with a skull in one hand and a scythe in the other, stood The Fool.

He was too late.

CHAPTER SIXTEEN

Nanette Eppling was a gravedigger. It was somewhat unusual to find a female gravedigger in the highlands of Scotland, and more unusual still, to find a gravedigger who enjoyed their work. But Nanette *did* enjoy her job. It fulfilled her entirely, and as such she always put extra, unrelenting effort into each thrust of the spade. That was probably why she hadn't been replaced with a machine. *Yet.* It was just a matter of time, of course. Besides, cremations — tacky and meaningless and denying of nature — were spreading from urban conurbations right into the heart of Scotland like chlamydia through a whore house.

But, a gravedigger. That's what she was, and what she'd always be. Sure, her husband wished she was in bed with him more often. And yes, she was exhausted by the time she had gotten home each morning — but she always found the extra energy needed to walk Abigail to school, before staggering back and collapsing into bed for eight wonderful hours.

Each night, as she started work on a new grave, the crunch of soil as her spade bit the earth sent an unfailing shiver skating down her back. It was the thought of being part of the great cycle of life and death. These pits would soon be filled by a deceased man, woman or child. In turn, the stomachs of many hungry creatures, whose homes were in the soil, would be filled (as well as providing fresh nutrients for vegetation). Then the birds and mammals would feast, and finally, humans would have their turn once more.

She recycled in a way very few people did, and she was proud of that. Nanette Eppling knew that one day, she would be part of the great cycle, and in a strange way, that thought comforted her.

Tonight, the soil was unforgiving against her spade, frozen and impacted by autumn's early surrender to winter's chill, but still, bit by bit, she chipped away at the hard earth. It was a new spot of land for her to be digging, recently acquired by St Matthew's Parish. It was a troubled area with a lot of fighting over this-new-drug or that-new-drug between various rivals — Nanette didn't really know too much about it. But she did know people went missing. Young people mainly, who had fallen in with the wrong crowd.

Clink clink click went the spade as it struck the mud time after time. *Clink clink click*

Clonk.

She'd only dug three foot down or so — about half of what was ideally needed — when the spade made the strange sound. A bit like when it struck rock, but *not quite*. She snatched her flash-light from her pocket; her cold, blistered hands fumbled for the button. When the light finally shone and pierced the darkness of the half-grave, she let out a shriek.

The recently bloodied body of a hard-faced young man was already rising out of the pit. Dirt fell from his shoulders in an avalanche.

A hand reached out for Nanette Eppling's throat.

Darkness.

For a long time, darkness.

Then, her eyes flicked open.

Where was she? What was that heavy weight pressing on her chest... *and why, oh why, couldn't she move her body?*

Pin pricks of light reached her eyes, but it wasn't enough for her to make anything out.

61

Clink clink click, went the familiar sound.

It was her spade. Only this time, she wasn't holding it.

Clink clink click

The little light that reached her eyes was snuffed out as more soil fell onto her. She tried to scream but the mud in her throat choked her passages.

Eventually, the clinking stopped. Minutes passed. She would surely die soon — surely suffocate.

Hours passed. Why hadn't anyone found her? Why wasn't she dead?

Days passed.

Why wouldn't she die?

Please God, she thought, if you have any mercy at all, please let me die.

CHAPTER SEVENTEEN

EXTRACT FROM THE JAMAICA OBSERVER, 26TH FEB, 2018

It is being 'reported' by certain tabloids that Obeah, a belief system that shares certain similarities to Haiti's Voodoo, is being practiced on the island with shocking results. Please do not be suckered in by the exciting false promises of myth or magic. The reports of two dead locals that have somehow come 'back to life' have been greatly exaggerated by other papers who are after nothing more than a cheap sensationalist headline. These two poorly people were simply misdiagnosed as deceased by an aged doctor, who has since resigned from his position.

That said, if Mrs Eralia Campbell or Mr Gerain Smith are spotted, please do not approach them and instead call the police. These individuals are dazed and confused and could potentially be a threat to all those around them.

In other news, more bad luck for island vacationers: the unusual cloud coverage that has blighted the island the last two days, throwing us into an almost night-time darkness, looks set to continue for a little longer yet...

CHAPTER EIGHTEEN

Christopher and Derek leaned back against the wooden boards of a closed stall. In the distance they could hear the rhythmic drumming of the Procession of Bones — a prelude to the parade that would soon be passing them by.

Christopher looked blankly at the grass beneath his feet. He'd failed again. His dad, first. Then Cassandra. Death. Himself — as always. Was there anyone he hadn't failed? How had his mother been coping since he'd died? All because he forgot to wear a helmet...

The funhouse had been closed since Death's demise, thick iron bars falling like teeth beneath its lips. Christopher had looked for another way in, but it was impenetrable. In truth, part of him had been relieved — he hadn't wanted to have tell Cassandra about her father.

Maybe if he could get Cassandra's missing bone back, and then find a way back into the funhouse... No. What would he do then? He had no... *magic*. No powers to create a being or to bring one back to existence, or even to snatch one out of a mirror realm.

"I know you're a bit down right now, but please *try* to look happy when the parade comes by," said Derek, his voice low.

"Hmm?"

"We've all got to look happy partner, or they will staple a smile onto our mouths faster than you can say Jack Robinson. Got it?"

"Sure."

"Show me."

Christopher let out a long breath, then tried to force his lips to widen.

"That's not a smile," said Derek. "That's not even an expression."

"I can't. Sorry."

The dark of the horizon flashed as fire breathers heralded the start of the Procession. There was music now — an infectious rumba that twisted its way around the beat of the drums. Singing, too. And dreadful laughter. Always, a dreadful laughter.

"You Goddamn will smile," said Derek, turning to Christopher and placing his thumbs either side of his lips. "There"—he stretched out Christopher's face into a broad grin. "Keep that going and we might just make it through this night."

"You could lend me your bandanna," replied Christopher, his lips already drooping out of the smile.

Derek grunted. "This"—he pulled gently at the red cloth around his mouth—"doesn't leave my face. *Ever.* Got it?"

"Whatever."

He could see them now, beyond the blue and red flames that the withered faces at the front puffed out and swallowed back in. Huge floats travelled behind them: the first was like a paper mache of a yeti type creature, but with writhing purple fur. *Worms*, Christopher realised in disgust. A gigantic locust stood upright on its rear legs on the float behind. Then a dragon, then a horned red demon. To the side of each of them were men and women dancing and spinning, their faces painted in luminous whites to look like smirking skulls. It was too dark to see their black clothed bodies, so the skulls bobbed up and down alone, grinning and laughing.

65

It was on the fifth float that The Fool stood. A living float made of a hundred intertwined people. His skull was raised high above his head, and the red and green paints shifted into series of zigzags, circles and pyramids. Behind him, propped high on a raised platform of bodies, sat a huge golden cage with a clutter of bones piled on its floor.

"Death..." Christopher whispered, trying his best to keep the embers of the forced smile between his cheeks.

For a split second, he thought he saw something happen in the cage. One of the bones had... *jumped*. Hadn't it? He stared hard at the cage waiting to see if it would happen again.

It didn't.

"Happy days, d-d-denizens!" began The Fool. "Tonight, for the first time in its h-h-history, The Carnival of Night will be moving! After the Procession, pack your bags, your stalls, and all your otherworldly b-b-belongings. The Carnival of Night is expanding! We've had slim pickings for far too long! Our t-t-time is now!"

A cheer erupted throughout The Carnival.

"What does he mean, *expanding*?" Christopher whispered, looking up at Derek.

Derek shrugged. "There's no Death any more."

Christopher frowned. "I know that, bu-"

"No Death means no *death*, partner."

"As in no death on... *Earth?*"

Derek nodded.

"But. So,"—he swallowed—"What's going to happen?"

Derek turned to him. "My guess: There's going to be seven billion more souls knocking on The Carnival's door, where ever that may be."

"Shit! What?! Derek, we can't let that happen. You know that, right?"

"What are we going to do about it, exactly? Ask The Fool nicely? I'm not spending the rest of my existence in a thousand tiny ribbons, and I'm not letting you, either. No, we're going to pack the Duck Shot up, and we're going to do exactly as The Fool says. Maybe the Titans will step in anyway. Not holding my breath, though."

"But—"

"We're not doing squat. End of."

Christopher clenched his teeth as the parade continued to march by. He stared at The Fool until his eyes strained to the point of popping, but the painted skull remained grinning as smugly as ever.

"I hate him," Christopher spat beneath his breath.

"Hush!" snapped Derek, glancing about him. "That's dangerous talk. You never know who's listening in."

He sighed. "Was it better here, before him? It must have been right?"

"With Bacchus in charge of the in-between? Hell, yeah! I'd take Bacchus any day of the-"

"Shh," hissed Christopher, putting a finger against his lips. "Did you hear that?"

"... Hear what?"

"There was a... a *grunting*, when you were talking. I don't hear it now, but I swear I did!"

"I didn't hear shit, and I don't think you heard shit before either."

"I did hear something! It was when you said, 'with Bacchus in ch—' there it is again! You must have heard it that time?!"

Derek's head cocked to his shoulder. "Okay. I *might* have heard something. But it was nothing really. Just the wind probab-"

"Bacchus," said Christopher, turning around to face the stall they'd been leaning against. He was fairly certain it had come from somewhere in there.

A grunt replied.

"Bacchus!"

Another grunt.

Christopher looked up at the sign resting on the boarded-up stall.

Coconut Shy. Closed.

Christopher knocked against the wooden boards. Then he pushed. Nothing was loose enough, or seemed at all likely to give. He began to shimmy around the stall.

"Where are you going?" asked Derek.

"Inside. I need to know what's making those noises."

"You're not going to find Bacchus in there, I can tell you that much. I've seen every head on that shy, and ain't none belong to a demi-God."

Christopher ignored him and instead carried on walking around the structure until he came to a wooden door with '*staff only*' sloshed on it, just like back at the Duck Shot.

Christopher twisted the handle.

"Shit!" He slammed his fist against the locked door. "I'm getting inside, one way or another." He took four quick paces back, before charging the door, shoulder first. He let out a yelp as he fell to the ground, his shoulder screaming. The door rocked very slightly, as if laughing at his pathetic attempt to break it.

Christopher gritted his teeth and got back to his feet. This time, he took six paces back.

"Might want to let me," said Derek, his voice reluctant. "If you're determined to get in, let's get you in with two arms still on ya." Derek drew a gun from his right holster and held it against the lock. Then he began nodding his head rhythmically, as if counting. It took Christopher a moment to realise he was nodding along with the drum beat from the procession. Every fourth beat, a larger drum would sound.

Derek waited...

...Waited.

There was a boom, a bang and a crack, all at once. Derek and Christopher stopped perfectly still, muscles clenched, for what seemed like forever. Surely someone had heard them?

But no one came.

Derek reached forward and twisted the handle.

The door creaked open.

CHAPTER NINETEEN

"I'll wait out here for you," said Derek, stepping aside.

Christopher paused a moment, then walked gingerly into the hut.

It was dark inside, and smelled of dust and rust and blood. A faint light from the ever-evening outside had followed him in and allowed him to at least trace the silhouette of the room: shelves laden with large, oval objects; brimming buckets on the floor, some filled with cloths, others with the spiked balls he'd seen thrown; mops leaned here and there against the wooden walls. Christopher's eyes slowly adjusted — the oval objects on the shelf gradually became vague faces. There were dozens of heads — far more than he'd seen on the stands outside. Spares, he guessed. His stomach turned as he saw a head that was just a smattering of skin on broken bone, the brain within protruding through gaps like a pink sponge.

Which one had he heard grunting?

"Bacchus," he repeated. His voice was quiet, as if afraid to disturb the many slumbering heads.

There was that grunt again. He span around to a shelf behind him, almost jumping when a pair or eyes flicked open.

"Who are you? What do you want?" croaked a male head with a black ponytail.

"Was it you?" Christopher asked.

"Was *what* me?" The eyes narrowed.

"It wasn't, was it?"

"You're not meant to be here. Leave now, before I scream for the boss."

"I'm not going to hurt you or anything, I'm just looking for someone. Something."

"Hurt me?" The head rocked back as it laughed. "You think you could hurt me? You have no idea what I've been through. You couldn't possibly even *conceive* a way to hurt me."

Christopher looked away, examining the other faces on the shelf. "Bacchus," he repeated. "Bacchus?"

He heard the muffled grunt at the same time as he saw the face. Or at least, what had *once* been a face. It looked like an old tin that had been kicked around and trampled upon, until it was so dented and misshapen that one would hasten to say it had ever been a tin at all. It had only one eye, with a swollen purple eyelid slowly lifting. Wherever the other eye socket had once been, pale skin had since grown over it, hiding it completely. Occasional patches of grey and blond hair sprouted out of its scalp like weeds.

There were no lips on the face, but there was an area of slit-skin near the base, that had a dozen or so stitches running through it.

"It was you, wasn't it?"

The head made that same muffled noise he'd heard through the thin wooden walls.

"I thought so." Christopher grabbed a spiked ball from a bucket. "Listen, I'm going to open your stitch-"

"HELP! BOSS! MURDER! **MURDER!**"

Christopher's body tensed. It was the pony-tailed head screaming.

"What the fuck is going on?!" croaked Derek, bursting into the hut.

"MURDERERS! HELP US BOSS! THEY'RE-"

71

Derek took a huge step across the room, grabbed a cloth from a bucket and stuffed it into the screaming head's mouth.

"Mpphpph," gasped the head. "Mphhh, Mphhhh!" Its eyes were wide and veins began to protrude all over its forehead.

Derek leaned into its left ear and whispered. The head became suddenly still and silent.

"We got to go, kid," Derek said, turning to Christopher.

"But..."

"Now!" Derek instructed, already half way out of the hut.

Christopher took a step towards the door, then turned. He snatched the misshapen head from the shelf.

* * * * *

"You're not keeping that thing," said Derek as he opened the door to his trailer.

Christopher followed him in. "It's not a *thing*. It's a person."

The head murmured its agreement.

"Whatever it is, you're going to dump it, or bury it, or whatever it takes to hide it. Anyone finds out we stole from another stall and... *shit*. Shit, shit, *shit!*"

"No one will find out."

"No one?" Derek laughed. "There were about forty witnesses to your thievery. I might have shut one of them up, but you think their boss won't be able to get any of the others talking? What the fuck were you thinking, grabbing it?" Derek's voice had lost nearly all pretence of a cowboy's accent.

"We need him! He knows something about Bacchus. Now, can you pass me a knife? Please?"

"..." Derek sighed. "Guess it's too late now anyway. Might as well hear what it has to say. But then, *it's going!* No ifs, buts or maybes. That thing is not staying anywhere near this trailer or my Duck Shot. Understood?"

"Understood."

72

"Mphhph."

Derek yanked open a draw and grabbed a paring knife, handing it to Christopher. "I think even you can handle a blade like this."

Christopher ignored him, instead placing the head on a table. It made a wet squidging sound as its open neck stuck down like a plunger.

Derek flinched. "Jesus, I eat off that table!"

"Well, maybe you should get some plates."

"It ain't easy finding good plates in this place!"

Christopher brought the knife's tip to the sewn slit on the face. He drew it across; the stitching popped rhythmically as if someone were pulling a zip, and the mouth fell open, rasping as it gasped for air. Christopher could hear breath escaping through its neck and nose.

"Uhhh. Rugh. Uhhhhh," it spat, half choking.

Christopher grabbed a mug and filled it with murky water.

"Drink," he instructed, tipping the head back slightly. It did, the liquid leaking out of its neck a moment later, thicker and tinged with reds and oranges. Christopher restrained a grimace. Derek did not.

"Is that better?"

"Ehh," it replied, its one eye open, watching him carefully.

"Can you talk?"

"Oo uhng."

Christopher frowned. "What are you saying? You don't speak English?"

"No one speaks English here," said Derek taking a seat at the table. "You not wondered why you can hear *everyone?*"

"I'm not speaking English?"

"Nope."

"Well... what am I speaking?"

"Damned if I know."

Christopher raised his eyebrows. "Okay, whatever. If that's the case, why can't I understand him?"

"Might be a lot of brain missing. I mean, that probably goes without saying, but"—he twisted the head around so that it faced him, then tilted it back—"yep, as I thought. He's missing a tongue."

"'Ats op ee eyin' oo 'ell 'oo."

"Someone sheared it off near the back of the throat. Just a stub there now."

Christopher sighed. "This isn't going to be easy, then."

"Hm. Give me a minute," said Derek, getting up from the table. He grabbed a leather boot from near the door, then pulled out another knife from the draw.

"What are you doing?"

"Just give me a minute, kid." The cowboy accent was slowly returning, Christopher thought.

Soon, Derek put a needle and thread down on the table.

"Ahhhh!" screamed the head.

"Relax," said Derek. "I ain't stapling you mouth shut. *As much as I'd like to*. Now, open wide for me. *Wider*."

Derek, with a slice of rounded leather in his fingers, placed his hand as deep into the mouth as he could. "This isn't going to work," he mumbled. "Look, partner, I'm going to have to do something a little... *unpleasant*. But it'll be over quick, capeesh?"

The head didn't have long to be scared; Derek snatched it up, cradled it in his left arm, then placed his hands in the mouth and yanked hard. There was a scream and a loud click.

"You..." Christopher began.

"Dislocated his jaw," said Derek, grabbing a spoon from the table. "He'll be fine." He squinted at the head. "You were a '*he*', right?" He placed the spoon upright in the head's mouth, propping it open.

"Now, kid, I need you to hold this piece of leather against what's left of his tongue, while I do the stitching."

"What?"

"Come on, get your dainty little fingers down that gullet."

*****

A pile of spit and blood had congealed on the table by the time Derek had finished.

"How's that?" asked Derek, yanking out the spoon and placing his hands around the jaw. There was another sickening click.

"Ughh."

"Better?"

"Ughj ...fink that's a lithle better," slobbered the head with a great effort, its leather tongue flapping like a mast in a storm, spit still dribbling down its chin. "But you are... *bastard...*"

Derek grinned. "That's fair."

"What's your name?" asked Christopher.

The head paused for a moment, its lonely eye flicking upwards into its skull, as if remembering such a detail was a great burden. "Me was... *Par?... Paddy!*"

"Paddy. Okay. You know something, don't you Paddy? About Bacchus. About what happened to him?"

The eye flicked up again. "Yes. Fink me remember something."

* * * * *

Derek had refused to come with them, opting instead to pack up Duck Shot and prepare for moving. He'd tried hard to persuade Christopher to stay with him, but it was an impossible task and eventually, he'd relented. Instead, he forced Christopher to at least take one his pistols with him — just in case.

The gun was hooked inside Christopher's belt, and he could feel it against his thigh with each step. Paddy, or what was left of him, was inside the bag on Christopher's shoulders, both of them silent as they snuck through The Carnival, towards the Forgotten Forest.

"Mmmph," came a noise from his bag.

"Shh," Christopher hissed in reply. "I made a few holes, you're not going to suffocate and, well, I'm sorry but we just can't risk someone seeing you."

"Mmmph!"

"It's not much farther. I can see trees in the distance now."

"Mmph."

Once inside the Forest so much as the view behind them was the same as in front — trees, trees and more trees — Christopher shrugged off his bag and took Paddy out.

"Okay, you're going to need to direct me from here."

"Mm. Let mes look 'round."

Christopher held Paddy out and slowly turned, until he completed a full circle. "Well?"

"Mm. Again. Turn."

Christopher raised an eyebrow, but rotated once more. Slower, this time.

"Stop. Stop! Back. Yes. Fere. Forward. Me went fat way first."

76

Christopher had more or less gotten used to the man's lisping accent during the story he'd told them in the trailer. There had been a great deal of pausing, and guess work by him and Derek to prompt Paddy, but eventually they'd gotten it all out of him. Paddy, long ago when he had a body to work with, had found Bacchus in the water of a ride that no one knew existed. Then, Chef had found Paddy. And then...

"Okay, good," said Christopher, walking cautiously so as not to trip over the forest debris. It was dark in The Carnival anyway, and out here in the woods... Well, it was worse.

"There. Take lefft at broken tree."

Christopher did. They came out into a clearing — a small circle of grass with logs littered haphazardly here and there.

"This where Paddy eat," said the head, his mouth dribbling at the memory.

There did seem to be a distant sound now. Static, almost. Was it water? "Do really believe Bacchus can help us, Paddy? Because Derek doesn't. Derek thinks if he was bested once, he'll just be so again."

"Bacchus help. Paddy sure! At least, maybe sure. I mean, me think."

"It was definitely *Bacchus* you saw in the water, right?"

Paddy paused. "Yes."

"Okay. Good. Just checking, because you seem awfully-"

"'Least, Green emeralds *look* like Bacchus eyes. Pretty sure."

"What?! You said you *saw* Bacchus in there — as in, *definitely* saw him!"

"Chef thought me saw something. I fink I did too. Why else Chef do this? Take right next here."

Christopher let out a long breath. "Uh, because you stole his ribs? That seems reason enough for a maniac like Chef to do pretty much anything."

"Only one rib. Keep this way going."

*****

It felt to Christopher like they'd been walking forever —
Paddy was clearly confused, and they'd looped back to the
clearing twice — by the time the roar had become clear and
distinguishable. By the time they found the rusting sign, its
painted letters flaking.

*TU NEL OF LOV . OUT OF O DER. DO NOT EN R, BY O
ER OF THE F OL :|*

Paddy rattled excitedly in Christopher's hands. "I told! I
told!"

There was an extra layer of gloominess to the ride's entrance.
Beneath them, grey wood chips sprinkled the forest floor as it
led them nearer to the sound of angry water.

"Still there. Pretty swans."

They didn't look pretty to Christopher. Their eyes were red
and their bodies black with mold and encrusted with dirt. They
lay on their sides abandoned and hopeless.

"In tunnel," Paddy instructed.

Christopher walked past the swans, staring at the raging
torrent to their side. If someone fell in that, there would
be *no* getting out. He gulped back his fear and continued along
the walkway at the edge of the water. Soon, the canal ran into a
dark tunnel... but the walkway that *should* have continued
along inside, was... *gone.* It must have long since crumbled into
the water, either decayed by time, or beaten to death by the
unrelenting waves. Either way, only fragments of it remained
now.

"*Shit!*" exclaimed Christopher. "Now what do we do?"

"Now you jump in the river, like a good little boy."

That wasn't Paddy's voice. A shiver ran down Christopher as he slowly turned.

Standing a few feet behind him, near the swans, stood the obese man from behind the coconut stall; he had a bag in one hand and a spiked ball in the other.

Next to him, his cleaver glimmering and his green tongue flicking, was Chef.

CHAPTER TWENTY

"Don't come any closer," Christopher commanded, pointing his pistol from one man to the other. His voice trembled as much as his arm; he tried to steady his aim by placing both hands on the gun.

It didn't help.

"I mean it. I will shoot you, so help me God, if you take even one step nearer."

Paddy's head rested by Christopher's feet, his one eye barely open, afraid to look, but also afraid not to.

Chef laughed. The sound was like someone trampling on broken glass. "Did you hear that, Haggis? The lad is going to shoot us!"

"Aye, I heard," grinned the obese man as he took a step nearer. "Once I'm done with you lad, we'll get Paddy's mouth sewn back up all nice and tight again. You'd like that, wouldn't you Paddy, you little bitch?"

They're already dead, Christopher told himself. *You're not killing them again, you're just... doing what you have to do.*

The obese man took another step.

Christopher closed his eyes and squeezed the trigger.

The gunshot rang out for only a moment, swallowed quickly by the incessant roar of turbulent waters.

He opened his eyes.

Chef was laughing. "He got you right in the chest, Haggis! Would you look at that?"

The fat man looked down; a surprised expression crossed his face. "Well what do you know? So he did." He placed a finger into the wound, rubbing it around thoroughly before bringing it up to his mouth. "Mmm. I don't taste too bad, if I do say so meself. Maybe need a tad more salt."

"*Now*- now stay back... or I'll fire again. I swear to-"

Haggis brought back his arm; the spiked ball whistled as it ripped through the air. It struck Christopher plum in the chest; the gun fell from his hands and he collapsed to his knees clutching his wound. His tee was ripped and beneath it, his skin was torn open. Hot blood was leaking out of him, dribbling down his legs.

Christopher gritted his teeth and lunged forward, stretching an arm out for the fallen pistol.

The next ball ripped the skin all along his arm, skipping up it and flaying inches, revealing sinewy tracks beneath. Christopher screamed.

"Sorry," whimpered Paddy. "So sorry. So sorry."

Haggis had another ball in his hand.

"Allow me," said Chef as he stalked over Christopher. He brought up the cleaver. "What can I get you Haggis, an arm or a leg?"

"Oh, a juicy leg for me, please Chef."

There was crack like thunder. Then two more bolts snapped the air. Chef fell down in a puddle of blood, three holes running through his forehead. Blood and brain matter squirted its way through the gaps.

"Derek... watch out!" gasped Christopher.

Haggis had already turned before the third bullet had hit Chef; a ball struck the cowboy on his gun arm. He didn't drop his pistol, but his next shot missed its target, hitting Haggis in his stomach. Derek tried to raise his arm to take aim again, but Haggis had charged him, tossing him to the ground. The fat man straddled Derek, pulling his arm back, a spiked ball in his hand. He brought it down hard onto Derek's face; there was a crack and squelch.

"You'll be pulp by the time I'm finished with you, cowboy." He raised his hand again and again and again.

Derek tried to fight back, tried to push the man off him. But the weight was too much, and his body was slowly becoming limp.

Christopher crawled forward, taking the cleaver from off the ground. With a tremendous effort, he lunged to his feet and sprinted across to the fracas.

The cleaver ran clean across the huge man's neck; his body went limp as he rolled off the cowboy.

"You— are—" gasped Haggis, as blood gushed out from his open neck. "Dea-"

Christopher raised the cleaver and brought it down onto the man's wound. He chopped four more times into the neck, until finally, he held the severed head in his hands.

He hobbled to the water's edge, tossing the appendage into the murky depths. Then, he walked back to Chef and began rolling the twitching body down to the water. Waves lapped at it, greedily reaching for it.

Calling for it.

There was barely even a splash as Chef fell into the water's cold embrace.

CHAPTER TWENTY-ONE

The wooden vessel creaked and groaned as waves lapped against its sides. In the far horizon, the setting sun doused the ocean in a goodnight glass of crimson wine. Derek didn't like wine. It took far too long, and far too much of it, to get the job done. No, he liked the turbid odorless liquid in the bottle he held in his right hand. That suited him — numbed him — just fine.

The patter of children playing below deck echoed up to him, as they chased each other in some game or another that could make no sense to an adult. His thoughts turned to his wife as a cloud darkened the horizon. What right did she have to leave him? To take *his* kids with her to Jack's, that treacherous woman-thieving bastard. His beautiful girls that he loved more than anything else in the world. No fucking right at all — that's what right!

The wind whipped the sail, cracking it and tilting the moaning boat to the side. There were screams from below as the boat rested on an angle, leisurely deciding which way it should fall. It decided not to capsize, at least not yet, and splashed down, rocking itself back onto an even keel.

"Daddy," said Amelia as she staggered up the stairs. Blossom and Callie trailed behind their elder sister; Callie's cheeks were soaked from tears.

"Mm?" Derek grunted. "What is it, my darlings? Did the boat give you a little scare?" He laughed and brought the bottle to his lips. "That's what it's like out here. You'll get used to it."

"Can we go home now?"

"Home?" he replied, momentarily confused. "*This* is home now."

"We miss mommy. *Please* can we go back. *Pretty please.*"

"I'm cold, daddy."

"There are blankets below," Derek replied, taking a long sip from his bottle. "You'll be fine."

The girls stood unmoving. "We want to go home, daddy," said Amelia, speaking up for her terrified siblings.

Derek rose to unsteady feet.

"You want to go home, do you?" His voice was accusatory, and his stinking breath leaked into Amelia's nostrils. "You want to go back home to your whore mother and her new lover? Is that right? *Is that fucking right?*"

The girls remained silent, apart from Callie who couldn't hold back her sobbing.

"Fucking ungrateful, the lot of you! Not wanting to spend some quality time with your old pa. You'd think you'd want to see what your daddy does for a living, and why he's away from home for so many nights on end. Your mother clearly didn't under-" He burped and staggered over to the wheel. "Fuck it. I'll take you back — but I don't want to see your faces again until we reach land. Understood? You sicken me. All of you."

"Daddy, we're sorr-"

"Get out of my sight!" he spat as he span the wheel.

* * * * *

A scraping noise woke him.

His vision was blurry and it took him a moment to realize it was daytime. The morning sun was far too bright for his bloodshot eyes. An empty bottle rolled down the deck landing against his chest.

He tried to remember where he was and moaned as it all drifted back: he'd taken an impromptu trip with the girls, surreptitiously 'borrowing' them when Caroline and her lover had been out. He just wanted to show the girls what he did — what a fisherman did — and intended to give their mother a little bit of a scare in the process.

There was that sound again. What was it?

It took him a moment to understand: it was that of wood fighting rock, but the rock easily winning. The wood was tearing and snapping and cracking.

He pulled himself up using the wheel for leverage, his face instantly washing pale as the situation hit him.

The boat was already uneven, the rear slightly sunken. He could hear screaming. *Children* screaming.

Derek sprinted below deck, his body smacking against the stairwell as the boat rocked chaotically. "Girls!"

"Daddy!" It was Callie's voice.

"It's okay, baby. I'm coming! I'm coming! Are your sisters okay?"

Another thud sent him flying down the last of the steps, his chin bouncing off the hard floor. He ran his tongue around his mouth; it tasted of blood and there were gaps in his teeth. He staggered back to his feet. "Girls! I'm coming. I'm coming!"

Tears streaked his face. What was he going to do — there was no life boat. He would have to make-

The next crack sent a huge fissure running down the center of the boat, the wood either side bending and snapping and splintering. Two huge planks fell in front of Derek, blocking his path. Water gushed in through every side.

"Girls!" he screamed as the sea filled the space around him, already rising to his knees. He didn't even notice how cold, how icy, it was.

"Callie?! Please tell daddy where you are — I'll... I'll come get you. It's going to be okay. *Oh God... Oh God. I'm so so—*"

CHAPTER TWENTY-TWO

EXTRACT FROM THE NEW YORK POST, 28TH FEB, 2018
UN-APOCALYPSE NOW

Three days ago our paper led with the following headline: *A Day without Death in NYC*

The article was boastful, smug, and worst of all, thoroughly naive. For that we apologize. But three days ago, a day without death seemed absolutely remarkable. Something to be celebrated, spread and recorded for all of history. It did not take long for the glimmer of gold to lose its shine. The very *thought* of a day without death now seems bleak and troublesome.

Imagine a world where cancer victims in their final stages seem to be stuck there indefinitely, in this terrible, agonizing realm between life and death. Car crash victims who are not just quadriplegic, but brain dead in any real sense, forced to linger — pulling their life support plug bringing them no release. Suicide is never the answer, in this paper's opinion, but now it's less so than ever as people are being found at home hanging from rafters, dangling alive like fish flapping on the end of a rod. How many are still waiting to be found? How many will *never* be found?

That is the world we are currently living in. It is not an imaginary cautionary tale constructed to warn those seeking immortality of the reality they are sugar coating inside their fantasies. It is simply the terrible truth of the world we live in right now.

What do we do with these people? The elderly that *should* be dead — should they be locked in their rooms in hospices until we understand what is happening? Should jail cells be emptied of criminals and these, for a lack of a better word, *zombies,* be contained inside instead?

The real question is this: what the hell is happening? Or to put it more fantastically, where is Death?

It has been hypothesized that the cause of this *un-death* is in fact some kind of virus. That these 'dead' people are indeed dead, but foreign organisms living inside them are keeping their bodies functioning, at least in certain, almost *mechanical,* ways.

More research is required in order to ascertain either the cause or the solution to this troublesome phenomenon.

CHAPTER TWENTY-THREE

Derek tried to open his eyes, but *he couldn't.*

"Right there, next," said a somewhat familiar voice. "Now push blade in. Yes, like that. Drag across. And... Twist!"

"God, I hope you know what you're doing..." Derek recognized that voice too. It was Christopher's. He sounded nervous. Why did he sound nervous? What was going on and why couldn't he remember? He tried to speak, but nothing came out. He tried to move his arms... they didn't listen.

"Of course I do know what I do! I fink, at least, I do. I was a doctor. I fink. Yes, that's it — twist! Well done."

"Oh God, is that meant to happen? Look at it all leaking out of him. Paddy, I swear I will play soccer with you, if..."

"Ahhh," Derek managed to moan.

"Derek!! Welcome back, partner!" shouted Christopher, far too loud for Derek's throbbing head. Why did the lad sound so damn happy?

"Told you, me good doctor!"

"Derek, can you understand me?"

"Yeee... " His voice was meek, barely a stretched whisper.

"Derek, listen," said Christopher. "I don't know how much you remember, but you got in a little bit of a... a *fight*, and well, we won, so that's good news. But uh... you took a bit of a pounding in the process."

"Uhhh. I..."

"We had to cut your head open — just a little, mind you. Your brain had swollen up and was pushing against your cranium. That's right, isn't it Paddy? Right. So, we've removed a little bit of bone here and there just to give it some extra breathing room. It was Paddy's idea, so you can thank him. You following, Derek?"

Derek put all his concentration into his right arm. He could feel it rising off the ground. He could feel his finger lifting.

"Look Christopher," said Paddy. "He's giving us a fumbs up."

"That's not his thumb..." said Christopher with a sigh. "But at least it's something."

"Now his eyes," said Paddy.

"His eyes?

"You going to need cut his eyelids. Too swollen for him too see."

"If you... if you..." Derek managed. He wanted to add 'dare' to the end of the sentence, but he couldn't quite manage it.

He felt the cold of the steel blade press against his eyes.

"Sorry Derek. But we have to get you fixed up, because we're going to need our cowboy to his *old* self for a while."

CHAPTER TWENTY-FOUR

Derek took a few cautious steps forward, then a few more, before his legs finally failed and he stumbled. He landed shoulder first against a fallen swan-boat.

"That was much better!" yelled Christopher, giving a thumbs up. "You're getting there now."

Derek groaned. "Yeah. *Getting there.* Look, maybe if I lean on you while we walk, I could make it back to my trailer."

Christopher bit down on his tongue. "Derek..."

Derek raised a hand. "Don't bother. I'm not sailing on"—he pointed at a swan—"one of those things, or on water that will tear me to shreds, just to *maybe* find a deity that has *already* been defeated once by The Fool."

Paddy, whose head rested on the back of an overturned swan near Christopher, let out a rasping sigh. "Me *need* you. Everyone need you. Living and dead. *Please.*"

"Keep your begging for someone dumb enough to fall for it. Now, one way or another, I'm going back to **my** stall. I'm going to pack it all up, and then along with the rest of the *sensible* beings in The Carnival who enjoy the use of a somwhat functional body, I'm going to follow The Fool." Derek hobbled away from the swan, his left leg dragging.

"Why do you do it?" asked Christopher as Derek passed him, heading to the ride's exit.

"... Why do I do *what?*"

"Why do you pretend not to care?"

"Because I don't. I *don't* care."

"Bullshit! You saved me from Chef when I first met you. You followed us all the way to here, just *in case* we ran into trouble — even though it meant getting yourself messed up in the process. Oh, you care, all right. You're just a stubborn old bastard who refuses to acknowledge it."

Derek turned and opened his mouth, then closed it again. Then opened it once more. "Yeah... well. Maybe I think you're going to cause trouble for the rest of us, if *I* don't keep you out of it. Maybe it's because I don't — *can't* — trust leaving you alone for five God-damned minutes."

Paddy rolled his eye.

"It's not just me you care about either. You care about humanity, too. I know you do."

"That's where you're wrong! Being human never did nothing for me, except bring me a pain I never asked for nor wanted." Derek turned and continued limping away.

"That's it. Go! Let Earth turn into somewhere just as terrible as this place. I mean, if *you* have to exist *here*, why shouldn't everyone else, right? Fuck the innocent men and women who-"

Derek stopped. "No one is innocent."

"What about children? Are they guilty of... of *what*, exactly? Of being born?"

Derek's touched his handkerchief. "I..."

"No. Keep going. Do whatever makes you happy. Give up on everything and everyone, just so you can keep on wallowing in whatever pit of self pity you fell into so long ago. I'll just... *I'll do it myself.*" Christopher stomped towards a fallen swan, placing his hands beneath it and heaving as he tried to flip it. His face reddened as he grunted and strained. The metal swan creaked as it lifted ever so slightly off the ground.

Christopher could feel his arms failing, his muscles tearing and burning — but it was his fingers that slipped first.

92

The swan fell.

Then, it didn't.

Christopher looked at the man who now stood by his side. He couldn't help grinning. "*Thank you.*"

"I'm not doing it for you, kid. Now, on the count of three, heave. One... Two... Three!"

Together, Derek and Christopher tossed the boat upright.

"Well, for whatever reason it is: *thank you.*"

The swan sat regally. Two large wings protruded from its side, blackened by dirt and time. Its metal neck towered into the air, rope dangling around it like a harness.

Derek put a boot against the side of the swan, then placed his hands on the left wings. There was a crack as it snapped off. A moment later, there was a second crack. He tossed the wings to the ground then limped to the edge of the forest, scouring the earth for something. He found what he wanted on a tree. A large grey branch dangled down, thick and straight and heavy. Derek almost hung off it, wrenching it with all his strength and weight: it snapped and thudded to the ground. The cowboy placed a boot on it and broke it in half again.

"What's he doing?" Christopher asked Paddy, the two watching from a distance.

"Me think Derek brain not quite fix. Maybe we need do more surgery."

Derek returned to the swan and grabbed hold of the rope around its neck. He took a knife from his belt and cut it in two, then grabbed the broken wings. A few minutes later, a pair of makeshift oars sat inside the swan.

Derek hobbled from swan to swan, cutting more lengths of rope away from necks — those ropes that still remained and weren't too badly rotted. He tied them all together and threw them in a pile into the upright swan.

"Are we ready?" asked Christopher.

"**We** don't need to be ready. Only *I* do."

"But you might—"

"Non negotiable. You get anywhere near that water, and I'm out of here quicker than you can say Jack Robinson."

Christopher was about to protest, when he saw Paddy staring at him, his eye moving left to right. "Let him, boy," said Paddy.

Christopher sighed. "Good luck. And... be careful. *Please*."

Derek nodded at him. "See you around, partner." He shoved his shoulder against the swan, sending it skidding down the decline, stopping at the flattened edge near the water.

Derek hobbled up to it. He leaned forward and peered over the bank, into the furious, turbulent waters below.

The warped reflection of a tired looking cowboy stared back at him, red handkerchief tied around his face, as if guilt could be hidden that easily.

He lifted a hand to the cotton and pulled it away from his face.

The reflection in the water changed, as its disguise was finally removed.

The fisherman who smiled back had three gaps in his lower row of teeth. Three reminders that he'd hidden for so long.

"Forgive me girls," he whispered, as he gave the boat a final push and leapt inside.

The current grabbed the little swan and threw it forward.

CHAPTER TWENTY-FIVE

The funhouse's mouth retracted its metal teeth as The Fool neared. A familiar, mechanical laughter greeted him as he stepped inside. He skipped down the metal floor, that, as if it knew what was good for it, remained flat and calm.

The Fool paused momentarily before entering the mirrored room, deciding to lean the object he held against the hallway's wall. Then, he entered.

The girl's body still lay on the floor, perfect in its pale stillness. It was like a waxwork. *A waxwork... A waxwork museum...* Yes, he liked that idea — the girl would be one of its star attractions. But no, that was for later.

He knelt down over the body, his beaked face nearing the corpse's. "So pretty. So very pretty."

A thud echoed around the chamber. The smudged outline of a pressed fist marked every mirror.

The skull laughed. "I h-h-hope you're having fun in there," he said, as the tip of the twisted beak touched the corpse's forehead. The metal nib creeped down over the cadaver's skin, all the way to its lips.

The mirrors misted up in a hazy breath; The Fool glanced up to see writing scrawled across them.

FUCK YOU

"Ahahahaha!" The Fool got to his feet, one hand on his stomach. "I d-d-do like you, Cassandra."

DEATH WILL GET YOU

The skull's mouth opened wide as if in shock; he brought a hand across to cover it. "Oh, my d-d-dear. Oh, you don't know! How terrible, how terrible, that *I* must be the bearer of such s-s-sad news."

Another breath fogged over the first, but no letters came.

The Fool raised a hand. "One second, my l-l-love." He skipped back down to the hallway to where he'd rested the object. He snatched it, and danced back into the mirrored room.

"B-b-bad news!" He laughed, holding the scythe in his free hand.

The clouded breath remained bare.

The Fool stepped to the nearest mirror and dragged a finger across the fog.

:(

"Now, I'm sorry but I must l-l-leave you, my little angel. For now."

The Fool left the hall of mirrors and continued deeper into the funhouse, past the shooting barrels and spinning disks, past the slide and wall of knives, until he reached the candled room.

The shadow was already waiting for him, shaking and shivering as it crept from wall to wall.

"Hello, Krios," said The Fool as he slumped into an ancient arm chair.

The ceiling above began to fade, and in its place *stars* flickered into life, forming constellations never before seen.

"The Gods grow suspicious," whispered the shadow, its voice warping and distorting as it crept about the room.

"Well w-w-what did you expect! Death to stop, and humans and Gods to simply... ignore it?"

"I cannot hide much longer. They will find me — and my siblings."

"P-p-perhaps you have all hidden long enough?"

"We are not ready for war with the Gods! We need our souls!" it hissed, the candles snuffing out as a cold breeze snapped over the room.

"*My* souls," the Fool replied, getting up. The skulls eyes began to glow. "This is my realm! You'd still be n-n-nothing without me. Still lost from existence. *Banished.*"

"Do not take that tone with me!" It was the sound of a thousand whispers rising to a cacophony of dread. But just as quickly as the voice had angered, it calmed. "*Do not* forget who made this possible for you," the darkness hissed. "And who can take it away."

The skulls eye sockets dimmed; The Fool waved a dismissive hand through the air. "Bah! We'll have our seven b-b-billion souls soon enough! Now, leave me. There's much that needs my attention, before The C-C-Carnival can leave."

The freezing air began to lessen its hold; the darkness relenting as candles flickered back to life and stars above faded to ceiling.

The shadow was gone.

CHAPTER TWENTY-SIX

The swan bucked as a wave swooshed beneath it, almost throwing Derek out. He grabbed an oar and got to his feet, standing near the front, counterbalancing the waves when he could, by shifting his body weight and leaning forward against the neck.

It took only a second for the ever-night outside to be replaced by the near total darkness of the tunnel as it swallowed up the little boat.

It was more difficult to navigate now, harder to see the waves coming. Derek had to *sense* them before they collided; he had to feel the swan move in advance as smaller waves, harbingers of those much more deadly, gave what warning they could.

"Oh, blow the man down, bullies, blow the man down!" he yelled out against the roar of water. A sea shanty he'd thought he'd long forgotten, that had risen like a phoenix in his throat. His face broke into a wild grin. He'd missed the rush, the excitement — the exhilaration! — of angry water. **"Oh, Blow the man down, bullies, blow him right down! Give me some time to blow the man down!"**

Shouldn't he have seen the green eyes by now? Derek recalled Paddy saying he hadn't walked far, before seeing them. Had the deity been moved? Derek hadn't noticed even a hint of green, and the boat was ripping through the tunnel like a drunken cannonball. Well, if he missed it, he was bloody well going to enjoy the ride. It was most likely going to be his last.

**"As I was a-walking down Paradise Street,
A pretty young damsel I chanced for to meet."**

A tremendous wave exploded into the swan, engulfing the crazed man clinging to its neck. When the water cleared, the man remained, still clinging, but with an even wilder smile now on his lips. He spat out water and continued his song.

**"I hailed her in English, she answered me clear,
"I'm from the Black Arrow bound to the Shakespeare."
So I tailed her my flipper and took her in tow,
And yardarm to yardarm away we did go!"**

There! He could see something — something green shining in the distance, and he was heading to it rapidly. He jammed his oar deep into the water on the right side of the swan; it swerved, skipping over a wave as it headed for the wall. The boat screeched and thumped against brick, metal scraping as it ricocheted again and again against the wall, almost flipping over, until—-

The boat jerked, then stopped; it bobbed up and down, but it no longer moved forward. It had become wedged between rubble once part of the crumbed walkway.

Derek leaned over the boat. Two green eyes shone like drowned jewels in the water only a few feet in front.

He tied one length of the rope around his waist, the other to the swan.

**"Oh, blow the man down, bullies, blow him right down!
Give me some—"**

He leapt off the boat, diving into the water; a freezing darkness engulfed him, twisting and turning him in its belly. He struggled against the hidden currents, trying desperately to turn around.

The eyes! They were mere feet away from him. He could see the silhouette of the body they belonged to, lit dimly by a radiant splendor.

Bacchus!

The current compelled him onward; he stretched out an arm for the God... Stretched further, further — his arm felt like it was going to tear off.

No!

He'd missed, and now he was tumbling past the deity.

He let out a gurgled anguished cry as he reached back, making one final grab.

His hand grasped at something solid.

Something metal.

It was a chain! He pulled himself against the current, inch by inch up the chain and back to Bacchus.

The small man was bloated and blue, his hands were chained behind his back and his feet to the stone ground. Bacchus's eyes darted around, following Derek with eager curiosity. With hope.

Derek's hand reached for his gun, but he realized as he touched it, that the spark needed to light the gunpowder would never ignite. Instead, he took the knife from his belt and began sawing into the first chain.

It took only a few seconds to realize that that too, was useless. Perhaps the chains were enchanted — it didn't really matter. All that mattered was he couldn't cut them.

He looked up at Bacchus. "I'm sorry," he mouthed, as he brought the knife to the deity's wrists.

CHAPTER TWENTY-SEVEN

Christopher sat on the bank, watching the water and waiting miserably. How long had Derek been gone? It was too long, that he was certain. Neither he nor Paddy had said a word since Derek had vanished into the distant tunnel. Christopher knew he needed to start considering what he'd do if Derek didn't come back, but God, he didn't want to. His head fell to his chest as despair's teeth sanpped at him.

"You hear that?" said Paddy?

Christopher looked up. "Huh? Hear what? Oh... the water... is the roar *quieter?*"

"It calmer now, yes. Me hear less swoosh, but me also hear something *else* too. Listen!"

**"...walking down Paradise Street,
A pretty young damsel I chanced for to meet."**

Christopher shivered. He leapt to his feet and gazed into the darkness of the tunnel.

"Oh, blow the man down, bullies, blow him right down!"

Emerging from the void of the tunnel, against the current and with its neck crooked, was a huge swan. And on it, oars in both hands and a crazed smile on his face, was the fisherman.

"Derek! It's Derek," yelled Christopher turning to Paddy and picking him up to see. "Look!"

Derek raised an arm in acknowledgment.

There was something else with him too, something lying sprawled out behind him.

He'd found Bacchus.

CHAPTER TWENTY-EIGHT

TRANSLATED EXTRACT FROM THE NOVAYA GAZETA, 2ND MARCH, 2018

(SUPRUNOV KORNEY'S FINAL ARTICLE BEFORE HIS DISAPPEARANCE)

The streets of Moscow run red tonight. The Bolshoy Bridge is slick with a red paste that lies beneath the squirming bodies, many without legs or arms, of the not-dead. The stench of limbs and burning skin reach out like a hand, cupping Moscow in its stinking palm.

One cannot help wonder if, somehow, this is Mr Putin's wet dream. One might, if given to cynical musings, wonder if it is in fact *his* doing — a desperate last gasp gambit to cling onto power. We are a country doused in blood that might as well be petrol, where a single match would be enough to start a raging inferno that would undo all positive progress our country has made in the last eighty years. "Military intervention has become a necessitation," said Mr Putin stoically, as he stood beside a resplendent T-90, imagining (no doubt) the phallic gun on the front as a metallic substitute for his own.

Your relatives, your friends, maybe even your children — upon death, they are taken to camps every bit as terrible as anything Hitler could have concocted. It is Hell on Earth, for these people. Yes, people. Their hearts might not beat, but their minds are still their own.

If you prick them, do they not bleed?

There was a time, not so long ago, that this great country was a *liberator*, where we saved Europe from the treacherous grasp of self-serving dictators. Will its once brave people now sit back cowering in their homes as we, as a country and civilization, crumble?

And the not-dead... Well, it goes without saying that they are not taking this lying down. They are becoming more organized. More aware. Only last night they broke into a khrushchyovka apartment block, slaughtering its residents and adding another thousand souls to their army. If your family were to become like them, would you want them relegated to a post-death camp?

Mr Putin, if you read this, please open negotiations.

Stop the madness.

CHAPTER TWENTY-NINE

Christopher helped Derek lift the writhing body out of the swan.

"Oh, I forgot just how good air tastes," said the naked man as they laid him down on the grass. "One becomes so used to water after a time." He was a pot bellied, at least middle-aged man, with dark, curly hair and large green eyes. His face looked much younger than the rest of his body — his skin clear and cherubic. But what Christopher couldn't help noticing — staring at — were his hands and feet. They were *tiny*, at least compared to the rest of him. Not much larger than a baby's, and they sprouted out of his ankles and wrists like hairs from a nostril.

"Has no one ever told you that it's rude to stare, boy," said Bacchus, his voice soft and lilting, even while chastising. "Not that it's the first appendage I've ever had to regrow... but still, manners *are*manners, after all."

"I... was just..."

"The only reason I'm having to regrow them anyway," the man began with a sigh, "Is because your friend there decided that I could make do without them. Thought it more appropriate than breaking my bindings, I suppose. And did he gently make the incisions? No! Hack, hack, hack!" He shuddered.

Paddy's eye opened wide. "Regrow? Uh, me need new limbs! Me need new limbs! Please, please,*please*!"

"Oh, how quaint. A decapitated head. Have a little patience, my egg-headed friend."

"I didn't have much of a choice," said Derek, as he shrugged off his shawl and draped it over the naked man. Steam rose from the soaking garment as it touched Bacchus's skin. "You ever tried cutting through bone? Tie that around your waist."

"I'd rather not."

"Oh, I insist," growled Derek.

"You mortals are so insecure," replied Bacchus. "Well, you'll have to wait a few minutes for my"—he clapped his tiny hands together—"limbs to grow back fully. These fingers are so uncoordinated right now. That is... unless you wish to tie it around me?"

"We can wait," said Derek.

"Very well. I could do with a glass of wine, anyway. For my nerves, you see. In fact, we could *all* do with a nice long drink, I'm sure. Now, be so good as to fill up one of your boots with water from that dreadful ride. I'll do the rest."

"I don't drink," growled Derek.

"Oh. How very dull."

"And neither do you, until this is all over. I didn't just risk my existence for an alcoholic— "

"Dipsomaniac," Bacchus butted in.

"—to start drinking again. You're going to help us overthrow The Fool. Then you can do whatever the hell you want. Party till eternity comes calling, for all I care."

"Ah," said Bacchus, his childlike grin finally failing. "I think perhaps overthrowing The Fool, might be a task a little too grandiose even for me. Our last encounter did not go ever so well." He glanced behind him at the water.

"Who is The Fool?" Christopher asked.

Bacchus frowned. "Well, you would have thought his son, of all people, would know that."

"Son?" Derek and Christopher said in unison.

"I see," mumbled Bacchus, chewing on his bottom lip.

"Son? Uh, no. He's not my dad." Christopher laughed nervously.

"Oh, but he very much is."

Derek tilted his head and stared at Christopher. "Is it true?"

"No! Of course not, Derek. I knew my dad. He was a good man. *Sort of.* His name was *Mark Dolus*. Markus actually, but no one ever called him that. He loved—"

"Is that your name too? Dolus?" asked Bacchus.

"Well, yes." Christopher's palms felt hot and sticky. "So you see, The Fool's not my father."

"Didn't do Latin at school, did you boy? Not that I can blame you. A rouges language. Now Greek... Ah! Language of the Gods. *Dolus* was a term used in ancient law. It means performing something *contrary* to a good conscience."

"I don't...

"A hoax, dear boy. Dolus means a *hoax*. A trick. A jape."

Christopher staggered back into a swan. "I- I know my father."

"Jupiter —*Zeus* also had a bit of a thing for mortals, before he gave up on everything. Many Gods do. Sometimes they have a need for a mortal's help, other times, for amusement."

"But my father was..."

"Took you to a lot of fairs, did he? Carnivals?"

"Yes... but..."

"You were just one the many spokes in the wheel, my boy. One of many! Your father used you to help set current events in motion."

Christopher slumped down against the swan until he was seated on the ground. "I don't understand..."

"How did you die, boy?"

"*What?*"

"Your death. How did you die?"

"... A car hit me. I was cycling and... well, I'd forgotten to wear a helmet."

"You wouldn't be in the in-between, if that was the case."

"But I am here."

"Exactly!"

Bacchus closed his eyes and whispered incomprehensible words. His lips hung sadly. "Oh dear. I see it now." He opened his eyes again and looked sympathetically at Christopher. "You'd been terribly depressed my boy, ever since that day at the carnival where you turned your back on your father. The day before he died in a plane crash, from which of course, his body was not recovered."

"I..." But nothing more came out. Bacchus was right. He *had* been depressed — of course he had! Who wouldn't have been? That day, the plane crash day, his world had gone from color, from full of hope and possibilities, to black and white and very sour.

"You didn't *forget* your helmet. A car didn't swerve and hit *you*."

"I..." Tears began to trickle their way down the grooves in his face. "I... *don't remember.*"

"It was all meticulously planned. Your depression. Your death. And, well, certain suicides *can* lead to purgatory."

"I don't remember..." Christopher repeated.

"*Why?*" Derek asked. "Why'd The Fool do it?"

"He knew Cassandra would bring him here."

"This... was all to get *her*?" said Derek. "There must have been an easier way. She would have brought someone else, sooner or later."

"He's a comedian, at least in his head," shrugged Bacchus. "To him, every act is vital to the great joke he's performing."

Derek walked over to Christopher and sat down by his side, putting an arm around him and pulling him into his chest. "It's okay, Christopher. It wasn't your fault. None of it. They weren't your decisions."

"Mortals rarely make decisions of their own." Bacchus shook his hands, then his feet. "Yes, these look far more fitting for a deity." Ever so slowly, he pushed himself up to his feet. First he tied the shawl around his waist, then with cautious steps, he walked over to Paddy. Bacchus placed both his hands on the head, and whispered again.

"There we are, my friend" he said, picking Paddy up and placing him on the ground. "It'll be slow, but it'll all grow back."

"Me... *get body*? Body for me? New?"

"Mmhm, a brand new body! Try not to lose this one."

Bacchus turned to Derek and Christopher. "He's stronger than me, The Fool."

"Who is he?" said Derek.

"I honestly do not know. A demi-God, perhaps. But he is powerful... I can't defeat him. *I'm sorry*. But! Good news is this: I can get us all out of here!"

"No," whispered Christopher, wiping a hand across his cheeks. "There's Death, still."

"Death?" said Derek. "He's gone. You know that."

"Gone?" asked Bacchus.

"The Fool destroyed him. He's just a pile of bones now, rotting in a cage."

"No," said Christopher. "He's not gone. I... during the Parade, I saw the bones move."

"A *cage...* Bacchus mumbled.

"You saw bones move?" Derek asked.

"Yes. I saw one of the bones jump, as if trying to get above another."

"Maybe the float went over a ramp," said Derek. "Because I think we have to face facts: Death isn't coming back from—"

"He's still with us," said Bacchus thoughtfully. "He can't form inside the Cage, is all. Yes, we're going to need his help. That is, if you really don't wish to leave — which I think you should at least consi-."

"We're not running!" cried Christopher, sniffing back his tears and getting to his feet. "So let's go find Death. Okay?"

"Not so fast, boy," said Bacchus. "If we all go, and The Fool is waiting for us... then it's over before it's begun. No, you and I, Christopher, shall find The Fool first, and we shall distract him the best we can." Bacchus turned to Derek. "And you..."

Derek grinned and tilted his head back, clicking it as he rocked it side to side.

"I've always wanted to be part of a jailbreak, partner."

CHAPTER THIRTY

The snapping of the tent flaps reached Derek long before the red and white stripes appeared out of the darkness. The wind had picked up since he'd left the others, but Bacchus had been certain — in the way only a God ever seemed to be — that the Cage would be waiting for him inside. The Big Top was on the outskirts of the Carnival, and it seemed to Derek that he'd been walking for an age. Surely the others had found The Fool by now. How long could they distract him for? Not very, he thought.

Derek was far more familiar with the huge tent than he would have liked to have been. It had often had the misfortune of hosting examples of The Fool's brutality; nights where the gathered crowd would sit around the center pit, baying for blood as they watched unlucky raffle winners be dismembered or de-constructed in some foul new way. Perhaps by a pack of crazed half-children, or maybe even by The Fool himself. On special nights, it would be by one of his new creations — terrible thrill rides for one person only. Rides you got on, but you certainly never got off.

The laughter of the skull still echoed in Derek's ears.

A single figure strolled back and forth outside the tent's entrance. A guard — that was a good sign. Maybe Bacchus was right.

The man was a little taller than Derek, and a hell of a lot wider, but that didn't worry him.

He crept tight around the edge of the tent.

The guard didn't notice Derek until the knife plunged deep into his neck, tearing at his throat. He raised his hands to push the blade away, but it was too late. His neck was already limp. A section of the man's own bone and blood fell into his hands. The guard tried to scream but only a managed a hiss, as blood misted the air.

Then the knife twisted like a corkscrew into his brain.

Thud

"Sorry friend," Derek whispered, stepping over the fallen body. "I'm sure they can get you all nice and fixed up when this is over."

The inside of the Big Top seemed vast without the rows of bodies filling the seats. Only a dim light lit the tent, a kind of golden hue, coming from an object in the pit-like area in the middle.

"Son of a bitch," whispered Derek. "You really are here."

The Cage sat resplendent on top of a high red podium, at the back of the circular area.

He waited a moment, watching cautiously for any sign of movement around him. Could there really have been only one man on guard? He waited as long as he felt comfortable, hearing only silence punctuated by the percussion of the flapping tent.

Derek hurried now — he'd wasted enough time on caution — down the aisle towards the pit, hauling himself over the raised barricade surrounding it. Inside the dusty red arena, he saw three tunnels, all covered with iron bars, where the 'performers' entered and exited the stage.

Derek had almost made it to the podium where the Cage sat, when there was a loud *thump*. Spotlights burst into to life, drowning him in shifting whites, yellows and reds. Twisted carnival music began wailing around him.

"Ah shit," he said, covering his eyes from the blinding rays.

"Welllllcome Derek Underhill, to tonight's spectacular!"

The voice erupted around him. It took Derek a moment, through squinting, bleary eyes, to find the person talking.

A man stood tall at the top of the seating area outside the pit, holding a megaphone to his mouth. He wore black trousers, a long red jacket, and had a top hat sitting at an angle on his head. The man's face was as pale as a skull, but his grinning lips looked like carelessly smeared blood marks.

Derek had seen the man before.

It was the circus ringmaster.

"And do we have a show for **you!**"

A *clink clink clink* made Derek turn; the bars covering the pit's entrances were lifting.

In the darkness of the center tunnel were three pairs of bloodshot eyes.

Derek grabbed his pistol as the dog-like creature hurtled towards him, snarling and spitting. Somehow, he got two shots off before it pounced on him, knocking him to the floor in a wave of dust, and sending his gun skidding away.

Jaws snapped at his neck; he pushed himself back just enough for the teeth to graze his chest instead, tearing only strips of skin. He could smell rotting death on the creature's hot breath.

The left head was limp, its eyes closed; blood dribbled out of its mouth — he must have gotten lucky with one of the shots. The central head opened its jaw wider than Derek would have thought possible. Saliva dribbled and stretched between its many rows of razor sharp fangs.

The creature lunged for his neck.

Derek screamed as he jammed his left arm, like a plank of wood, between the creature's closing jaw. It felt as if thick needles had been glued to a clamp, piercing and crushing him in equal measures.

113

The creature opened its blood-dripping jaw. His arm, or what remained of it, fell limply to the ground.

The second mouth snarled as it stretched open; a snake like tongue crawled over its lips.

Derek needed to reach his belt — to grab his knife — if he was to have any chance. But the creature's belly lay flat against his. There was no getting his arm between them.

His vision was blurred and swirling; all strength had leaked away from him as if the wounds in his arm were holes in a boat.

This was it. He was sinking.

He was going to be lost for eternity.

Derek closed his eyes and muttered a final, silent prayer.

He hadn't *meant* for his tongue to brush against his teeth, but it had done so. Time seemed to stop as he felt each of the three gaps. As he saw each of the three faces, and heard each of their voices.

A new determination ran through his body. With every ounce of strength he had left, he rocked his body as far to the right as possible, his torso becoming as taut as a stretched elastic band. Then, he let go. His body rolled to the left, forcing the creature to keel over with him.

Derek snatched his knife with his right hand; the dog was still on its side as the blade pierced its belly.

He stabbed again.

And again.

The creature let out a final, mournful whimper, before it stopped wriggling and writhing all together.

For a moment, Derek just lay on his back, breathing slowly.

"And now for tonight's main event!" boomed the voice through the megaphone.

"What next..." Derek croaked, as he forced himself to his feet and staggered across to his gun. His left arm lay limp and useless by his side; rays of light shone clear through the wounds.

He turned to look at the gates, waiting.

"May I present, Frankenstein's monster!"

The *thing* didn't come out of one of the gates. *It came out of all three.* It burst through them in a wild tempest of splintered wood.

Derek stepped back as he took it all in.

"Jesus Christ..."

It was a... a gargantuan *person*. But, it wasn't just one a person. It was made up of at least a hundred people. It's legs and arms each consisted of a dozen broken, twisted people, somehow mashed together. Bones jutted and ripped through skin on its stitched torso and face — if you could call it a face — and its whole being wailed in pain as it walked.

Laughter ran through the megaphone, as the carnival music changed key, its pace increasing to a crazed, warped frenzy.

The creature stomped towards him, the floor beneath shaking with each huge step.

Derek raised his gun and steadied his arm the best he could. He pulled the trigger; the bullets ripped through tiny sections of its head, through eyeballs that marked it like acne.

He shot again and again, until soon, he had only one bullet left.

The creature was still coming.

"Last bullet's always a keeper," he said. "For emergencies only."

The laughter grew louder, the music grew faster

Derek spun on his heel and pulled the trigger.

The laughter stopped. There was a distant thud.

Derek allowed himself a grin before he turned back to the creature. "Just you and me now, pal." He dropped the spent weapon on the ground and took his knife instead. "And if it's going to end like this, I'm going to scratch you up something real bad, before I go," he growled.

The shadow of the monster's fist engulfed him as it raised an arm high into the air above.

Derek lifted his knife as he waited for the inevitable.

Then, he waited a little longer.

Longer still.

The brute's arm *wasn't falling*. Or at least, not all of it was. *Bits* of flaking skin and organs were floating down like ash. Wisps of *people*.

"What the hell..."

The creature staggered backward, as its body began to fall to pieces. It let out a hundred howling screams, as it became nothing more than a vast spiralling plume of dust.

Derek coughed, as the remnants of the creature stung his eyes and throat.

Finally, the mist of flaking skin began to settle, and in its center, where the creature had been stood, was a cloaked figure holding a scythe.

Derek glanced up at the cage. It was *still* on the podium, and the bones *still* littered its floor.

"Huh?"

"I hope you don't mind," said the figure. "As I, well, I'm certain you had it under control and everything, but we really are in a rush."

CHAPTER THIRTY-ONE

"Where are you? Where are you? *Where are you?*" repeated a frantic Edward, as if chanting the words might teleport Death to him. He paced back and forth in the hallway area outside his boss's door with a thin sheen of sweat dribbling over his face. Edward removed his spectacles and dabbed at his cheeks with a handkerchief. Coming from inside the room, he could hear the constant *clunk, clunk, clunk* of new scrolls tumbling out of tubes and into whatever space they could find.

Death had been gone too long. *Far* too long. Earth was starting to look like hell. Not literal Hell, of course, but it was getting pretty grim. There were already more than seventy million souls that needed to be collected, that were instead wandering unfettered amongst the rest of humanity, some confused, many angry. Angry over their fate. Angry over how the rest of humanity was treating them.

Edward opened the door a crack, only to be met by a wave of scrolls tumbling out and swamping his shoes. "Oh dear," he muttered, as he tried to squeeze the door shut — but now that it had gotten a taste of freedom, the wooden portal wasn't having any of it. Edward groaned as he gave up, glancing instead down the hallway behind him. He scurried along it until he came to a golden object protruding from the wall.

"Desperate times..."

Never, in his many hundred years as Death's apprentice, had he had to use the horn before. Yes, he had had to motivate Death on many occasion, as the ever increasing burden of

117

humanity weighed heavy upon his shoulders. Death's motto, in all its menacing splendour, used to be: "I have come for your soul, —insert name here—". Now it was, "So, what are the amenities in this place like? Good area to retire to?"

Exotic teas and coffees that Edward procured on his own rare trips away, had placated Death for a while — and they still helped, somewhat. As did the amusing little trinkets for his desk, like the marbles on strings, that rocked back and forth, back and forth. What had helped most of all though, and what had kept Death going in the end, was the suggestion of starting a family.

Not only had he become as doe-eyed as an amorous deer, upon seeing his daughter, but as Cassandra had grown, her amazement and fascination with life and death, and all that came before and after, had helped Death see his own job with new eyes.

Edward gripped the horn in one hand and then placed his mouth to the rim.

"Will"—he gulped—"Will the sorting office *please* stop sending Obituaries to room One-Zero-One. Death is out of office. Repeat, Death is out of office. Please redirect to storage temporarily. Thank you."

He walked back to Death's door and listened. The clunking had stopped — that was something. With a sigh, he slumped down against the wall and considered.

Why hadn't Death come back? Surely something couldn't have happened to him, and yet, what other option was there? And where were the Gods in all this? Had they finally followed Zeus and abandoned humanity?

Edward made a decision. A decision that, he knew, might result in him losing his job and being sent back to the underworld. An *executive* decision, he thought, as he flicked more sweat from his forehead.

He marched down the corridor until he reached the lockers. Death might need a change of clothes, after all. Who knows what mess he's in! Edward ran his fingers over the blue suits, then the green suits, the pinstripes...

He stopped on Death's ancient cloak.

He couldn't. *Could he?* He was only part qualified but... it would be *fun,* to surprise Death dressed in that.

Edward pulled the garment up over his head, and then grabbed a spare scythe.

A wave of excitement washed over him.

He was going to The Carnival.

* * * * *

"You can't be serious?" said Edward, pulling back his hood.

Derek tipped the — now open — cage over. The pile of bones spilled out onto the red dust.

"I'm absolutely serious." He pointed at the bones. "That right there, is Death."

"Oh dear," said Edward, getting to his knees. He found part of the cranium and placed it upright. "This isn't good at all. Sir? Sir, can you hear me? Just... *rattle,* if you can hear me."

"Derek, by the way," said Derek with a nod. "Thank you for what you did. You kind of..."—he ran his good hand through his hair—"saved me."

The apprentice turned his head. "I'm glad I could be of assistance! My name is Edward. How do you do?"

"How do I do *what?*" Derek replied suspiciously.

"Oh erm, I meant, how are you?"

"*How am I?* How do you think I am?"

Edward examined the cowboy. His face was scarred, his chest clawed and bloody, and part of a left arm hung lame at his side.

119

"Maybe you're a morning person," said Edward, turning again to the bones.

Derek snorted.

"Sir? Are you still in there?"

click

Edward's brows raised as he turned on all fours, looking for whatever had made the sound. It took another click before he found it: two tiny, connected finger bones — no, *toe bones*, were bending back and forth.

click click click

"Sir! Thank goodness! We'll get you back together right as rain in no time at all! You just trust me sir, nothing to worry about."

"How long's 'no time at all'?" Derek asked.

"Oh, just a few hours, I suppose. Essentially, although his soul is still connected to his bones, he has to learn to reform his essence, to restructure his body and to-"

"We don't have hours. We have *minutes*."

"Before what, exactly?"

"Before The Fool does this"—he pointed at Death's bones—"To Bacchus, and something worse to my friend."

Edward sighed. "I'm very sorry, but that's not my—"

click click - click click - click click click click

"Sir? He did that to *Cassandra?*"

click

"Oh, I'm... I'm so sorry."

click - click click click click

"But I'm not even half trained!! I'll only be a-"

click!

Edward gulped. "... Yes, sir." He reached out and gingerly took hold of a rib bone, placing it deep into a pocket on the side of his cloak. He then got back to his feet and pulled the hood down over his face, shrouding it in shadows.

"Take me to The Fool."

CHAPTER THIRTY-TWO

It was as the eerie glow of the funhouse crept into view, that Christopher noticed, for the first time since entering The Carnival, that the moon was shining. It was pale, and no more than a slither in the shape of a sickle. Or the end of a scythe, he thought. A second later, a thick breath of clouds covered it completely, once again draping the Carnival in darkness.

The twisted lights of the funhouse were vivid in the conquering darkness.

Christopher paused. He could once again see that day, years ago. His father beckoning him to follow. Calling to him. Only, he wore a different face now. Painted.

Come on. It'll be fun. I promise.

I promise.

Promise.

The memory of that moment had echoed in his mind for three years. It was like an out of tune piano playing in the back of his skull; sometimes the notes were quiet and slow, sometimes they boomed out in a deafening knell, mournful and tormenting — but they were always there, if he ever just allowed himself to listen.

But today, it played a new song. The sound of a fist falling across the keys.

Iron teeth covered the funhouse's mouth.

I promise.

Ha!

Hahahaha!

Christopher made his own promise. Today he would lay a ghost to rest.

"I'm part God," Christopher considered. He hadn't meant to say it out loud.

Bacchus turned. "What's that, my boy?"

"I was just thinking... if The Fool is my father, then that means I'm part God. Is that why I could see Cassandra?"

"I suppose so. But I'm not even certain that The Fool is a God. In fact, I think it unlikely."

"A demi-God?"

"No. Something else, I think. *Something new...*"

Christopher frowned. "What?"

Bacchus stood in front of the bars and clapped his hands. They began to tremble. To shake. Christopher thought, as they began to turn green, that they were rotting. He couldn't help grinning as Bacchus pulled back the arms of dangling of Ivy and motioned him to pass through.

"That's very novel," said Christopher, as he dipped between the plants.

"I'm somewhat a novel God," Bacchus replied, following him through. "But I'm quite handy to have around, I like to think." The darkness of the hallway was lit a shimmering green that radiated from the God's eyes. A mechanical laughter cackled around them.

Christopher didn't jump. He didn't even shiver.

The distant sound of metal waves began.

"Brace yourself," Christopher warned, as the first herald of the oncoming tsunami approached. "This is where things get interesting."

But Bacchus wasn't bracing himself. Instead, he was leaning down with a palm against the floor.

The metal ripple began to slow, grinding to a halt just before Christopher. As he watched, grass began to explode out of the metal hump, tearing holes clean through it.

The wave was, in a matter of seconds, a miniature hill in a long strip of green.

"What are you, the God of rustic scenery or something?"

"Come along," said Bacchus, ignoring him and stepping over the tiny incline.

Christopher trailed behind, as grass continued to sprout and grow. "You said he's not a God."

"Hm?"

"The Fool. You said he's something new."

"Ah. I do not think a demi-God could defeat me, even when I *was* steaming drunk."

"You were drunk?!" Christopher yelled more loudly than he'd meant to.

"I'm not the God of greenery, boy. And I do have a slight weak spot for a good red."

Christopher raised his eyebrows and let out a long breath. "So, what is The Fool then?"

Bacchus chewed on his tongue for a moment, before answering simply, "I don't know."

"But you *think you know*, don't you? If not a God, he must be *something*."

Bacchus sighed. "Fine. Fine! But this is just a guess, mind you. What do you know of the Titans?"

"Titans? Not a lot. One holds the world on his back, right?"

"Ah, Atlas. Not *the* world, but all worlds in fact. The Titans were the creators of the Gods. Their parents, if you will."

"So... The Fool is a Titan, then?"

Bacchus raised a hand. "Wait, will you my boy! I'm not yet done."

Christopher ran a hand through his hair. "Sorry. Go on, please."

"It is said that The Titans — as was the universe itself — were born of Uranus. Uranus was a cruel entity, every bit as petty and malevolent as the worst stories you humans have about us Gods — yes, don't worry, I've heard them all. But Uranus, as terrible as he was, was *nothing* compared to his son Cronus. Cronus was the most powerful of Uranus's five children, and tired of his father's reign, rose up against him. He castrated his own father with a sickle, and banished him for all eternity. Under Cronus's dictatorship, excuse me, *reign*, a long period of peace known as the Golden Age began."

"Sounds, okay, I guess. So, what happened?"

"Same old story! Cronus grew fearful of his children, believing that they would one day overthrow him, as he had once done his own father aeons previous. Cronus, however, was determined not to make the same mistake that his father did. So as his children were born, he devoured them."

"*What?*"

"He ate them. Devoured means *ate*."

"Yeah, I know what it means, it's just.... Okay, whatever, keep going."

"All but one were devoured who, with the help of Cronus's sister Rhea, survived. She smuggled him away after he was born and hid him from Cronus until he was ready. That child was Zeus."

"So, Zeus eventually overthrew Cronus?"

"Firstly he freed his brothers and sisters from Cronus's stomach. Then began the Titanomachia — a war between the Titans, and their children, the Gods, that shook the universe to its foundations. But, the Gods eventually overcame their parents, banishing those they fought to a realm of darkness called Tartarus. Not all of the Titans, mind you. Some fought *with* the Gods, and some did not fight at all. But most, especially those loyal to Cronus, were sent away."

"I don't understand. Are you saying The Fool was a Titan, but that he wasn't banished."

"No. I believe The Fool is a demi-God... *and* a demi-Titan. He is a mongrel breed. A hybrid."

Christopher swallowed. "Who were his parents?"

"I don't know. I can't even guess. But I think perhaps he plans on reuniting them. He plans to punish the Gods that banished his parent — Zeus is already missing, after all. I believe he is crafting an army of souls to fight the remaining Gods." Bacchus looked at Christopher, a smile returning to his lips, his voice softening. "Or perhaps I'm wrong about all of this! Perhaps he is simply a demi-God who got lucky, finding me in a bit of a stupor."

Christopher tried to smile back. He couldn't. What did this all mean? Was *he* part Titan, part God? He certainly didn't feel it!

Cassandra's body remained untouched in the room of mirrors, not rotted or aged a single moment since he'd last seen it.

"That's her. That's Death's daughter. She's... she's trapped in the mirrors here. Please, is there anything you can..."

Bacchus knelt beside the body. He sighed. "No. This isn't a complete vessel. She is part of Death. This body is *not*. It is just... *a body*. It might as well be a doll. I'm sorry."

Christopher looked at the mirrors, searching for a misted breath.

Nothing came. His head fell.

"Then... what can we do?"

A voice echoed around the room. Mocking and gleeful. "*You c-c-can always b-b-urn, child.*"

The hallway beyond the room lit up in a volcanic red. Christopher saw in the harsh light, the skull's mouth opening. Fire was growing within.

The ball of flame twisted as it exploded out of the mouth, hurtling towards him.

* * * * *

Bacchus was suddenly between the flaming ball and Christopher. He grimaced as he caught it in his hands, squeezing it until it began dripping. Soon, there was a puddle of water on the floor, and nothing left between his palms.

"Hide," whispered Bacchus as another fireball careened towards him.

"But—"

"Now!"

Christopher hesitated a moment, before dashing behind a row of mirrors.

There was an explosion this time, as the fire hit Bacchus. The God staggered back, his chest and arms scorched.

The Fool stepped out of the passage. "I had so wanted to k-k-keep you whole for Father. But I see now that *that* idea was somewhat impracti-c-c-cal."

"I don't think you'll find me so compliant, today," said Bacchus.

Christopher could see the God's eyes in the mirrors — the green was intense. Growing. The room itself was becoming engulfed by brilliant beams — as if they were bombs ready to-

The room rocked. Glass screeched as it cracked and shattered. Christopher felt stabs of agony in his back and legs, as broken glass bit into him. He fell to the floor, pain almost overwhelming him. And yet for some reason, his mind kept jumping back to the face of the pale girl he'd met on the bus. That pretty, pale face.

The light dimmed; Christopher tore out shards of dripping red mirror from his legs; he pushed himself to his feet and staggered over to the now kneeling God.

In the hallway opposite, The Fool lay on the floor, motionless. A scythe and skull lay silent by his side.

Bacchus was breathing hard, his skin was torn and his eyes were fading to darkness.

"Bacchus!" said Christopher, grabbing his shoulder and helping him to his feet. "Are you okay?"

"I... I will be, thank you my boy."

The laughter exploded like thunder; it rocked the room, and the glass on the floor danced in glee.

Christopher turned. The Fool's body was already on its knees, the laughing skull in one hand, a scythe in the other.

"Oh dear," said Bacchus, as insects crawled out of the skull and took to the air in a blizzard of black.

Bacchus screamed as the swarm began to eat him alive, tearing at his flesh and muscles. His body tried to regrow — *to heal* — but they were devouring him faster than he could manage.

A handful of the insects leapt off the God and onto Christopher, biting and ripping the flesh from his back. He fell to the floor, rolling as he tried to squash them.

"AHAHAHAhahaha," laughed The Fool. He stood over Bacchus now. A huge green tongue leapt out of the skull's mouth and crawled over the floor to the God, twisting around him, wrapping him completely.

It took only seconds for Bacchus to be engulfed, and when he was, the end of the tongue fell out of the mouth.

For a few seconds, the tongue pulsed and wriggled, as if the God inside was trying to escape.

Then, it stopped.

Christopher got to his knees, ignoring the pain of the insects. He felt an anger rising in his belly. A furious hatred for his father. For all the terrible things he had done to Christopher, and to everyone else he had ever known and cared about. The creatures around him continued biting at his flesh, gnawing at his skin, as he rose to his feet once more, and as the anger swelled within him, seeping into his arms.

Rushing into his hands.

Into his mind.

His soul.

"*Fuck you, dad!*" he screamed as a wave of energy rippled out of him, throwing The Fool against the wall. Pieces of glass speared the Fool's body.

The Fool was silent for a moment. There was a look of surprise on the skulls face. Of more than that - of shock. The paints that covered it began to run, dripping down onto the floor.

Christopher bent over, panting. For a moment, he allowed himself to believe it was over.

Then the wailing began. A laughter unlike any that had come before. The sound of pure malice, a sound sickening to hear. The body grabbed its fallen belongings.

"P-p-priceless!" the skull stuttered, as a globe of red began to build within it.

The ball hit Christopher like a bull, throwing him to the floor, melting the skin on his chest.

For a moment, all he saw was blackness. His head swam in a desperate dizziness. His limbs were limp and his body didn't respond.

129

The Fool was upon him, swinging his scythe back.

"Goodbye, *son*! Ahahahahaha!"

Christopher tensed his body and squeezed his eyes.

There was a *clink*.

The screech of metal on metal.

He opened his eyes to see the shrouded figure of the reaper, its scythe hooked against The Fools, yanking it back.

And behind him, was Derek.

* * * * *

The Fool hissed as he turned. "You?" he said as he stared at the cloaked figured.

"Not quite," came the figure's reply, as did its fist, swinging up against The Fool's chin, connecting hard just below his pointed beak.

The Fool staggered back, his mask twisted at an angle.

Derek leapt at him, plunging his knife deep into the body. The skull screamed as the hand released it and it fell to the floor. Derek stabbed the body again, twisting it into the chest cavity.

Edward pulled back his hood.

"Who the h-h-hell *are* you?" chattered the skull.

"Just a messenger," said Edward, raising a boot above the skull. "And my boss says, see you in-"

Edward hadn't felt the sudden chill in the room. Hadn't noticed the darkness above, as the ceiling had been pricked by a thousand tiny stars. A dozen constellations. A dragon... a blade... *a sickle*.

The shadow shivered as it danced across the wall, as it stretched across the floor. As its arm lifted out of the void and wrapped around Edward's neck.

Christopher tried to warn him, to scream. To do anything! But his body betrayed him and left him helpless to only watch.

Edward yelled as the shadow pulled him down into the darkness. As he struggled against it, something fell out of his pocket, tumbling near Christopher. *A bone.*

Christopher watched in shock as the cloaked man was swallowed by the void.

He was gone. Both him and the shadow. Gone.

The stars began to fade.

The ceiling returned.

Derek had turned in time to see Edward pulled into the floor. But he'd looked away for too long; a twisted metal beak pierced his neck, spearing him and lifting him off his feet.

Christopher tried again to move, desperate to — but his body was frozen. He watched instead, as Derek slid off the hooked beak and collapsed onto the floor. The Fool's body was on him, its beak stabbing and twisting into his chest.

Christopher tried to look away, as tears ran down his face. "I'm sorry," he said, his voice not even a whisper. "I'm so sorry."

The glint of single piece of broken mirror caught his eye.

It was misted.

Fogged.

There was no writing on it, and perhaps it hadn't been to do with Cassandra at all, and yet... a slight *feeling* began to trickle back over his body, like someone throwing a single cup of water into a dried up empty well. It wasn't much, but...

He began to crawl through the broken glass, dragging his broken body until his hand grasped the bone Edward had dropped.

Blood streaked the floor as he crawled further, through glass and fallen insects, through numbness and tears, through all the pain he'd ever felt in his life.

Until he reached the body.

The skull was laughing. Derek's screams had died to whimpers.

Christopher could feel electricity pulse through his hands as he placed the bone into the split torso.

Then his weary eyes began to shut.

Darkness.

Silence.

Was... was that a voice? A *girl's* voice?

Christopher's eyes flickered open to see a pale faced girl holding a skull high above her head.

Then his eyes fell once more, as the sound of something shattering into a thousand tiny fragments echoed around him.

CHAPTER THIRTY-THREE

Christopher sat on top of the hill overlooking his hometown. Smoke still drifted up from some of the more ruinous buildings. Almost a hundred million not-dead, in total. And all of them just...*died again*, at the same time last night — as if their souls had been ripped from their bodies. The papers had their own theories about viruses, immune systems, airborne cures and a hundred other possibilities. But Christopher knew that Death must have had a very busy night.

He brushed the back of his head, still half expecting his hand to fall into the gash that he'd gotten so used to. But it was just hair brushed over scalp.

He was glad to be back home. His mom had cried and fussed, and then cried some more. "Thank God! I thought you'd been taken to one of the camps!" He'd cried too. He hadn't meant to, or even thought he would. But he had. They were different tears now, too. Not tears that dribbled out because of an emptiness inside, but tears that were pushed out by a feeling that had been missing for a long time.

"Mind if I join you?" came a soft voice from behind.

Christopher turned his head. "Cassandra?" His lips burst into a grin as he got up and wrapped his arms around the pale faced girl.

"Really? We're doing hugs now?" Cassandra said with a roll of her eyes, but there was a smile skipping up her lips. "How very human. I thought you might be above all that now."

"What are you doing here?"

Cassandra sat on the grass and gestured Christopher to join her. "I've been given the night off. It's been a long process for us. Not just delivering souls, either — you wouldn't believe the paper work that comes with it. And without the help of..." her voice trailed off.

Christopher nodded. He knew who she meant.

"You must be glad you're back!" Cassandra said, trying to sound more cheerful. "Not many leave purgatory. Gods though... well, dying was never *your* destiny."

"How's Derek?"

"He's good! Great, in fact. Since he's been in charge, they've torn down each and every ride and turned the whole of the in-between into a giant rodeo. You should see Paddy on the bull! Now he's got legs, he-"

"A rodeo!?"

Cassandra began to laugh. "I'm kidding! It's not a rodeo. Yet. But it is a much more pleasant place to visit now. Somewhere for lost souls to find themselves. I'll take you sometime. Just to visit."

"I'd like that."

They sat for a while, as the orange sun began to fall beyond the horizon.

"What happened to Bacchus?" Christopher asked. "He wasn't inside The Fool's tongue, so where did he go?"

Cassandra shrugged. "No idea. He'd just *vanished*. Unlike Edward, who my father believes was taken to Tartarus, Bacchus is just... *gone*. As if he chose to leave."

Christopher ran a hand through his hair. "Are they going to be able to get Edward back?"

"I don't know. My father thinks there will be war soon, though. That the Titans are rising. And without Zeus to lead the Gods..."

Christopher's head dropped.

"Hey, don't worry. It may never happen. And even if it does, maybe it won't change anything here."

"Or maybe it'll be the end of everything everywhere."

"... Hey, I've been meaning to ask you something."

Christopher looked up. "Yeah?"

"Is that a ladder in your tights or... or *what?*"

"Huh?"

"On the bus. That's what you said when you walked over to me. What's the rest of it?"

"Oh." He could feel his cheeks glowing. "Is that a ladder in your tights, or the stairway to heaven."

Cassandra laughed. "Is that your best chat-up line? Kind of apt, I guess. The heaven part. I don't wear tights."

"Yeah, I kind of noticed."

"I've been meaning to ask you something too..."

"Oh?"

"Yeah." Christopher smirked. "How the heck do your dad's bones move with no tendons to pull them?"

Cassandra just smiled. She leaned her head against Christopher's shoulder, and for a while longer, they watched the sun dip down.

A high pitched whine disturbed them.

"Hey kitty!" said Cassandra, gesturing to the ginger cat with her fingers. "Come here, come here. Aw, Christopher, look! Poor cat only has three legs."

It gingerly approached Cassandra and rubbed its side up against her leg, before looking for further attention from Christopher.

He ran a hand over the cat's back.

"Cassandra. You know you can come here whenever you want. My mom makes a decent stew."

"Oh, don't worry, I'll be back. And hey, you can come see me some time too! You're a part God-Titan thing after all, you better start learning how to use— Hey, look at that!"

"At what?"

"The cat. Look!"

"I don't see—" Then, he did see. The stump where the cat's fourth leg should have been was *growing*. Christopher was certain of it. As he watched, a tiny paw was forming on its end.

Cassandra frowned as she looked up at Christopher. "I didn't know you could do that."

"Neither did..." A finger of goosebumps traced its way down Christopher's spine.

He suddenly remembered how The Fool had fallen silent, when he'd said 'dad'.

What was it Bacchus had said to him, after they'd rescued him from the water?

It was all meticulously planned. Your depression. Your death. And, well, certain suicides can lead to purgatory.

"Christopher? What is it?"

Was he just a spoke in a wheel? Had Bacchus known that he, along with Derek, would one day save him — or was this all just part of something bigger?

"I... I don't know. Nothing that can't wait, at any rate." He forced a smile.

Cassandra leaned her head back against Christopher's shoulder. "So... you can *heal*. And I can reap. We're like life and death. That's pretty cute."

"Is that *your* best chat-up line?" he replied, as in the distance the sun finally gave way to darkness, and a sickle moon above ushered in the night.

The end.

Thank you for reading.

For more of my work, and to follow the sequel as it is written, please visit http://reddit.com/r/nickofnight

34223792R00083

Made in the USA
Middletown, DE
24 January 2019